ANGIE AND THE FARMER

A Historic Western Time Travel Romance

Susan Leigh Carlton

Susan Leigh Carlton
Tomball, TX

Susan Leigh Carlton
Tomball, TX 77377
www.susanleighcarlton.com

Publisher's Note: This is a work of fiction. Names, characters, places, and incidents are a product of the author's imagination. Locales and public names are sometimes used for atmospheric purposes. Any resemblance to actual people, living or dead, or to businesses, companies, events, institutions, or locales is completely coincidental.

Angie and the Farmer/ Susan Leigh Carlton. -- 1st ed.

Contents

Time travel used to be thought of as just science fiction, but Einstein's general theory of relativity allows for the possibility that we could warp space-time so much that you could go off in a rocket and return before you set out.

Stephen Hawking

Description

A western historical Oregon Trail Romance of 39,000 words, or around 150 pages. It is a clean story with one non-explicit sexual scene between a married couple. The heat level is 2 or rated GP.

Angie Thornton met Jed Lewis after being swept downstream in a flash flood. She was found by a small boy from a nearby wagon train on a tree limb in a tree beside a creek.

Jed Lewis, the eighteen year old son of one the rescuers, was immediately smitten when she first came to the train.

With 2,000 miles remaining on the Oregon Trail, will Angie be able to overcome her reluctance to accept help? Can she find love with Jed, a farm boy from Ohio?

What did either of them have to do with an iPhone found in a 90 year old grave?

If you like Angie and the Farmer, a review would be appreciated.

Author's Notes

Visit www.susanleighcarlton,com and sign up to be notified of new releases and to receive drafts of the first chapter when I start a new book.

This is a historic western romance. It contains one non explicit sexual scene between a young married couple and has a heat level of 2.

There are several journals in museums where the women recorded each day's events, giving distances traveled, water availability and grass. Some of the references I use came from the emigrant journals kept during their travel. I used fifteen to twenty miles as a day's distance depending on the terrain. One journal account detailed the passing of seventy trailside graves on a small portion of the trip. I purchased copies of the journals to use in my research.

Statistics tell us that one in ten travelers died during the trip. With over 400,000 emigrants using the trail, that is a lot of pain, suffering and death. Very few of the deaths can be attributed to clashes with the Native American Tribes. Accidents and illness were the cause of most, with cholera standing out as a cause.

Caravan, train, and company are used interchangeably as names for the group. The people on most trains passed rules and elected officers.

I used terms that were common in the day. For example, receipt is what recipes were called. Another thing to note, is Angie speaks using twenty-first century terminology and idioms while the others are using 1867 terms.

The iPhone was introduced on June 29th, 2007. In the story, I said one hundred forty years, it was actually one hundred thirty nine.

The First United Methodist Church of Salem, Oregon:

Following the precept of John Wesley to take the gospel to people everywhere, the Methodist Foreign Missionary Society sent a mission to the Indians of the Pacific Northwest in 1833. The next year the Reverend Jason Lee, Jason Lee's nephew, Daniel Lee and teacher Cyrus Shepard traveled overland to Fort Vancouver. At the urging of Hudson Bay Factor Doctor John McLoughlin, they selected a headquarters site in the Willamette Valley about ten miles north of the present city of Salem. Today this site is preserved as Willamette Mission State Park.

Regular church services began in the Mission in 1835, but it was not until 1841 when headquarters was moved to the Salem location, that the Methodist Episcopal Church of Salem was formally organized.

Jason Lee was one of thirteen charter members and David Leslie became the first pastor.

The so-called cutoffs on the Oregon Trail, such as the Sublette Cutoff, and the Lander Cutoff were usually discovered by trappers and followed old Native American Trails. They were taken to bypass difficult passages, but some saved many miles of travel. The Sublette-Greenwood Cutoff shaved eighty-five miles or about seven days off the journey. It came at a price in that it required them to trek forty-five miles with no access to water, very little wood for cooking and poor grass for their animals.

Prologue

Haynes Falls, Oregon April, 2016...

Haynes Falls Mayor Wilton Chastain held the ceremonial silver shovel he would use to break ground for the badly needed new Meriwether Lewis High School.

"My friends, it is my great honor to signal the beginning of construction for Haynes Falls' first new high school in nearly a century. This is a momentous occasion and I do this with great humility."

He tried to push the shovel into the partially frozen ground with no success. He put his foot on the top of the silver-plated shovel and applied his considerable weight to the task, and managed to penetrate the frozen earth about three inches. He turned the shovel over and dispersed the dirt.

"Let the construction begin," he pronounced in a sonorous voice. The eleven attendees dutifully clapped, and as a body, hurried to get out of the bone-chilling wind coming from the mountains.

The heavy equipment began excavations the next day, filling the air with a choking blue smoke from the huge diesel engines. At noon the next day, everything was halted.

"What do you mean stopped?" the bombastic mayor shouted at the project manager for the new school.

"Mayor, we dug into a grave," the engineer said.

"Whose grave? The environmental study didn't show any cemeteries on the property."

"I know, sir. But we broke into a grave."

"Well, move it then and get on with the work."

"It's not that simple," the engineer protested. "The gravesite is protected by law."

"What law?" the mayor demanded.

"The Oregon Legislature passed OREG CODE ANN § 22-3-802 in 2011. I'll read part of it; 'preservation in place is the preferred policy for all human skeletal remains, burial sites, and burial material; and (f) notwithstanding any other provision of law, this part is the exclusive law governing the treatment of human skeletal remains, burial sites, and burial materials.'

"It pretty well spells out our course of action, Mayor. We have to stop and get the state medical examiner involved. It's not going to be quick or easy."

"Get the City Attorney involved. It's about time he earned his keep."

"It's going to cost a fortune for the heavy equipment just sitting there, not to mention the men."

"That's the construction company's problem, not the city's."

"Their position is it's our fault for not doing our due diligence on the impact survey."

"Give that to the lawyer too. Do you have any good news for me?"

"Not at this time," the project manager said.

"I should have stayed where I was, then I wouldn't have to put up with all of this crap," the mayor replied.

The construction site was turned over to the Oregon State Medical Examiner. Two weeks later, he held a press conference. "We have determined the remains are those of an unidentified Caucasian female and have been in the ground for over ninety years, therefore, there will be no criminal actions regarding this case. I will be issuing a ruling of death by natural causes. I will now accept a few questions."

"What happens now?" a reporter for the Haynes Falls Herald asked.

"We have invited the Oregon Preservation Society to participate in the next phase of the investigation, which will attempt to determine identification of the decedent."

* * *

Two days later, KNHF's Breaking News featured video accusing the examiner's office of stonewalling the media on developments at the gravesite. The State Examiner's Office said they could not comment on an ongoing investigation.

Two days later…

"This just in," a breathless street reporter announced on a Salem TV station. "KSAL News has just learned an iPhone has been found in the mystery grave at a construction site in Haynes Falls. We are concealing the identity and voice of the source since they are not authorized to speak for the Medical Examiner's Office or the Preservation group.

"Our source informs us the iPhone and other items found at the site have been sent to Apple Labs in Cupertino, California for analysis in an attempt to identify the victim. We will continue to bring you updates as they become available."

Three weeks passed…

KNHF Evening News, Breaking News…

"The mystery of the grave found at a construction site in Haynes Falls deepened today when it was learned the iPhone found in the unmarked grave on the site for the new Meriwether Lewis High School was registered in December, 2014 to a Miss Angela Thornton of Brevard, Missouri. Miss Thornton and her family were thought to have died in a flash flood. when one of the Missouri River tributaries swept the family car away in 2015. The bodies of the parents were recovered, but their daughter's body was never discovered. A source in the Examiner's Office revealed their investigation had determined the ground around the grave had not been disturbed in decades and the casket had not been opened prior to being pierced by the excavator.

"The source said a plea for relief from the City was granted, and construction can proceed, provided the remains are buried in the original location and the site preserved and protected."

CHAPTER ONE

Jedadiah Lewis

Steubenville, Ohio, 1865…

Hiram Lewis was offered a princely sum for his farm near the Ohio River by the Steubenville Coal Mining Company. That night, he discussed it with his wife, Sophronia.

"Sophie, I'm going to take them up on this. We'll likely never get another chance like it."

"Well, I'll tell you, I just don't see the need for us to go through selling this place and starting over with another one just like it," she said.

"I don't either. A good many folks have been talking about going west like that Greeley fellow said back in '65.

"Whereabouts west?" she asked.

"I was thinking California or Oregon."

"Land sakes, Hiram, that's all the way on the other side of the country."

"It is. I was listening to a bunch of fellers talking about it down to the store the other day and they said it would take about seven months to get there."

"Seven months? That means Jed and Mandy would miss out on the last part of the school year."

"Mandy is eighteen and she'll be getting married soon, so she won't need any more. Jed has had enough schooling already, so it's time for him to do regular work."

"Jed's only seventeen. He's still a boy," she said.

"You had just turned seventeen when we got married," Hiram reminded her.

"Times have changed since then, Hiram."

"Not so much. While I was gone to the war, things kinda got bad around here. Everybody is in the same boat. If we don't take the money, someone else will. This is our chance to start over. It will be an easier life for the young'uns than it would here. Besides, I'm tired of the bad Ohio winters."

"You're the man so you make the decisions. When would we go?"

"We would have to leave in March, so as to make it through the mountains before winter."

Resigned to the fact, she said, "I guess we would need to start getting ready, deciding what to take and all."

"I already started looking and asking. I'm thinking we should plan to get two braces of oxen, and a big wagon. I spoke to a man yesterday who is planning to go to Oregon. He's joining up with five others that will leave here the middle of March. I kind of signed us up for it."

"You've done all of this without even talking to me first?"

"The chance was there so I took it. I've got a list of what he recommends we have. We'll restock things along the way if we get low."

"What's on the list?"

He handed the list of staples to her. She read it aloud. "600 lbs. of flour, 120 lbs. of biscuits, 400 lbs. of bacon, 60 lbs. of coffee, 4 lbs. of tea, 100 lbs. of sugar, and 200 lbs. of lard, sacks of rice and beans, dried peaches and apples."

Hiram said, "The bacon will be in large barrels packed in bran so the hot sun will not melt the fat. I'm also taking a rifle, a shotgun and my pistol. We'll be taking a plow, shovel, scythe, rake, hoe; and some tools. I got some seed for corn, wheat and other crops.

"There's another thing, Sophie. We can't take all of our belongings, only what's necessary, and then we can get new things when we get there."

"Will we have enough money to do all of that?"

"Yes. It's an awfully good price for the land. There's coal underneath us and they're going to sink a coal shaft here so they were willing to pay."

"Papa and my brother worked in the coal mines in Pennsylvania. I think it shortened Papa's life and Micah's not doing too well right now either. Papa was only forty-seven. I tell you, I hate the idea of Jed working in the mines and that's what he'd wind up doing. It's the right thing for us to do.

"I'll tell them about it come morning," he said.

* * *

Mandy was clearly not happy with the news. "Why do we have to go all that far?" she asked.

"It's our chance at a better life," her father told her. The government gives you free land; all you have to do is live on it five years. Between your Ma and me, we can claim two sections, and Jed can get a section when he turns eighteen. When you get married, you and your husband can claim the same amount."

"Papa, how am I going to get married? I won't know anyone out there. What about Calvin?"

"Has he said anything about marrying up with you?" her mother asked.

"No, but he will."

"When?"

"I don't know."

"I never favored him for you anyway," she said. "We're going to leave the end of the second week in March. If you're determined not to go, I'll speak to your Aunt Mabel and see if you can stay with them."

"Aunt Mabel? I can't stay with them."

"Then you best think on it.

"How do you feel about this, Jed?"

Jed was excited. "I think it's great. I can help drive the wagon and all. It's going to be a real adventure. Since it isn't likely there will be another war, I can hardly wait."

Later…

"Mama, I can't live with Aunt Mabel and Uncle Jake," Mandy pleaded.

"Why not?"

"Uncle Jake has grabby hands. He tries to touch me every time we're over there. He's always hugging me and bumping me, making it look like an accident and such."

"Why haven't you told us about this?"

"Papa would have been real mad, and I didn't want any trouble. I just wasn't going to be alone with him. Don't tell Papa. I won't say any more about not going."

Jed went with his father when he purchased a new wagon, a spare axle and a spare wheel to be slung under the wagon, called a prairie schooner. They also purchased eight oxen. Hiram planned to add at least two horses also.

Jed was curious about the choice. "Papa, oxen are slow. Wouldn't we go a lot faster with horses?"

"That's a good question. In fact, I asked the very same thing. They told me horses would be faster, our speed will be limited by the cows anyway. We would need to carry a good bit of grain to keep the horses fit on the trail. That would take up space in the wagon we need to store our provisions. The horses aren't as strong as the mule or oxen and they are more likely to stray or be stolen by Indians.

"They also said mules can last longer than the horses and are more surefooted in the mountains, but we would have to take some grain for them too.

"He recommended oxen They are a little slower, traveling only 15 miles per day on average, but they are more dependable, and less likely to run off. The Indians don't bother them as much. Oxen can stand the long trip and can get along on the what grass there is along the way. They are less expensive to buy, but they will be more useful when we get there. We got these eight for less than $150.

"Oxen are a lot easier to harness too. We'll save a goodly amount of time getting to leave every morning.

"It isn't going to be easy. You and I will be walking a big part of the way and it'll be easier to keep up with the oxen."

"Why do we have to walk?" Jed asked.

"It lightens the load the team has to pull. Your mama and sister will walk quite a bit, but they aren't as strong as we are, so they'll ride some."

"You sure have been studying up on this, Pa."

"I've been thinking about it for a good while now, so I've asked a lot of questions, especially with those that are going."

"Have you known any of them long?"

"I was in the War with two of them."

"I wish I could have gone to the war."

"No you don't. It was a horrible experience."

"But you won," Jed said.

"Nobody wins a war, son. There are only losers."

CHAPTER TWO

On The Way

Jed and his father loaded the wagon with the things they had purchased and those they had in their home. Room was left down the center for Sophie and Mandy to sleep. Jed and his father would sleep on bedrolls under the wagon. They said goodbye to their neighbors the night before and were ready to go come morning.

The Lewis wagon along with five others left Steubenville before first light on March 14th. It was dark when they set out, with Sophronia and Mandy in the wagon, and Hiram leading the four oxen in harness. Jed was in back with their two horses, the oxen and three milk cows. The third day out, one of the wagons left them and went back to Steubenville. Three days later, the remaining five arrived in Zanesville. Hiram and the other men located a company in the process of forming up. Hiram paid the joining fee and became a part of Major Clint Adams's wagon train. The next day, the wakeup call came at 4:00AM. The women were out of bed and fixing breakfast while the men rounded up their livestock from the center of the circle, and harnessed their oxen or horses and began moving. Their first day on the Oregon Trail had begun.

The sun was dipping low on the horizon. "How far have we come today?" Jed asked his father.

"A little less than we did on the way from home. I imagine it's about fifteen miles, why?"

"My feet are tired. When will we stop?"

"That's up to the wagon master," Hiram told him. He looked at the sinking sun. "It won't be long now. We'll stop before dark. Your mama will have to fix dinner, while we get the cows milked and the oxen unharnessed and taken care of.

"Look up ahead. Clint's giving the signal to circle the wagons now."

"There's no Indians around here, why circle?"

"The wagons will serve as a corral and the animals won't be as much trouble to round up in the morning."

"We didn't do this before," Jed said.

"It's kinda hard to circle five wagons."

Jed grinned. "I guess it is. Are any more of ours turning around and going back?"

"I don't know. We have a long row to hoe ahead of us. I keep wondering whether it's the right thing to do myself. I was pretty sure before we left. I'm just wondering if the women folk are up to it."

"Ma's strong; she'll be all right. I don't know about Mandy," Jed said.

There were thirty wagons in the train now. During the day they spread out instead of traveling single file, and avoided breathing so much of the dust stirred up by the other wagons. The days turned into a sameness across the flat Ohio and Indiana countryside. Fourteen days later, the train stopped in Greenfield, Indiana.

Clint Adams called a meeting. "Folks, we're going to lay over here three or four days to give the stock time to graze and rest their feet."

"What about my feet?" one of the men called out

"You can rest them at night." There was a collective laugh at the wagon master's humor.

"Whilst we're here, tend to any repairs you need and restock your larder if necessary. I'm going to get the blacksmith to come out and check the hooves of my animals and anyone that needs him can make the same arrangements. I don't know what he charges, but it's up to you if you want to or not. He's going to check mine, for sure. Check and grease your axles and make sure they're tight. We got about six weeks to get to Independence."

"Jed, we're going to be here three or four days," Hiram told him. "We need to check the wagon and the harnesses real good. We don't want to break down on the trail. You'll have a chance to rest your feet some. Look at your shoes, might be a good idea for both of us to get an extra pair.

"I want to have the hooves of the oxen and horses checked to make sure their shoes are tight. I'll get the blacksmith to check them while he's out here."

"Yes sir."

The oxen and horses had been checked and received the necessary treatments. The supplies had been replenished and loaded into the wagon. The last chore Jed had was to grease the axles the day before they left.

A cold rain was falling so it was not possible to have hot food before the wagons broke camp. Cold biscuits and honey was all they had for breakfast. Jed and his father were both wearing slickers while Mandy and her mother were able to remain relatively dry. The signal came to begin moving. The train was single file on the muddy road due to the wet fields. Dust would not be a problem this day.

The rain stopped around eleven thirty and the sun came out shortly after, lifting Jed's spirits. The end of the day was welcome after a day of slogging through the mud.

Sophie had purchased a journal and pencils in Greenfield and decided to keep a record of their days ahead. The first entry described the rain and mentioned Jed had caught a cold. The entries for the next two days told of the sneezing and coughing. Sophie wrote, "Mrs. Parnell gave Jed a potion. I don't know what it was, but it made him drunk."

Another entry read, "Jed is better and is walking with the animals today. Mandy is walking too. I will have to start walking too. Come the mountains, we'll all walk."

Six weeks later…

"Independence at last. A week's layover. Looking forward to that," she journaled.

In addition to the Adams caravan, there were three others ahead of them. Independence was the jumping off place for most of the trains headed west. Major Adams held a driver's meeting. "Everyone should get all of their needs attended to while we are here. Fort Kearney is just about the only thing between us and Fort Laramie and it isn't nearly the size of Independence. We'll be two and a half weeks to Fort Kearney and around seven or so to Fort Laramie. Fort Laramie is our halfway point to Oregon. From Fort Laramie on will be hard going, with mountains and rivers to cross. If you're thinking of turning around, this would be the place to do so. This is my third train, in seven years, so I know what I'm talking about."

"We'll be crossing the Mississippi one week from today, weather permitting. It will be a ferry crossing."

Four days later…

The train had stopped for the day. The widow Hannah Scoggins was preparing the evening meal when her seven year old son, Jeremy, asked permission to go down to the creek that would be their source of water.

"You go ahead, but don't go in the water."

"Yessum." He took off running. Jeremy always ran.

CHAPTER THREE

Angela Thornton

June, 2015…

Angela Thornton was born in Brevard, Missouri, on January 27, 1998. The apple of her father's eye, she grew up a tomboy on the family dairy farm outside Brevard. The old Oregon Trail crossed what was now their farm, and left wheel ruts from the thousands of wagons that had passed through seeking their fortune in the western paradises praised in the newspapers.

Even though she was one of the prettiest girls in school, Angie's focus was totally toward earning an athletic scholarship. She had no close friends except for those on the basketball or volleyball teams. In spite of her mother's pushing, she never had a boyfriend. She wanted good grades to help her chances for a scholarship. "Angie, there are other, and more important things than sports," her mother told her.

"I'm not interested in them right now," Angie said. "I have to get a scholarship."

"Your world is too small. You need to let others in."

Always an athlete, Angie led her high school's volleyball and basketball teams to the Missouri Class 3A championship two years in a row. She was a familiar sight to the fans of the high school basketball team, her long strawberry blonde ponytail bouncing from side to side as she flew down the court and pulled up to hit a jump shot. She was also on the swim team and had been a lifeguard at the community pool for two summers.

Angie had offers from eight major schools in volleyball and basketball. She wanted to play both sports, but most coaches discouraged the dual activity, and preferred their scholarship athletes to focus their attention on one sport.

She used her fifth and last NCAA official visit to go to the University of Nebraska in Lincoln. "I'd like to play volleyball and basketball. How do you feel about that?" she asked the Huskers basketball coach.

"It's been my experience that volleyball can make a good basketball player better, providing they have the stamina required. The physical demands on a player for a good team are heavy, and the Huskers are good in both sports. It's hard to excel at both, but if a girl wants to try it, I have no real problems with it; however, she should ask herself if she wants to be good at both or great at one."

"What about great at both?"

"That's a tall order. I know you were outstanding in high school, but the girls playing college ball were all number one on their teams in high school. Volleyball and basketball are both considerably faster at this level."

"You don't sound encouraging," she said.

"We are a top ten team nationally. Our goal every year is to be number one. Our girls work hard."

"You're losing three starters this year," she said.

The tall female coach grinned. "You've done your homework. We are losing three, but we had the ninth best recruiting class in the country last year," she said. "We'll be good again this year. If you want to be part of it, we'd love to have you.

"We have a good volleyball team too. The coach is a good friend of mine and he will tell you the same thing I'm telling you. At a Division Two or Three school it would be less demanding, but at D1, it's tough. We'd like for you to be a part of the Husker program in any case."

On the way back to Brevard, Angie sat in the back seat, ear buds in and read a book on her iPhone. The spring rains had taken the mighty Missouri out of its banks as well as the feeder streams. The current in the creek following the path of the highway was fast and the water was rising. A dip in the road had water flowing across the roadway into the creek.

Angie's father, Barry had already slowed the Lexus below the speed limit when he hit the water. The Lexus fishtailed, and when he over corrected, the car went into the creek. The water quickly rose to the level of the headlights. The force of the current caused the car to break contact with the streambed and it began to move. It moved faster as it was swept away by the rapidly moving water.

"We've got to get on top of the car and hold on," he yelled.

The force of the water made opening the door impossible. Angie felt the car hit the water, and yanked the buds from her ears. "Dad, I can't get the door open."

"Open the windows, before the battery dies," he said.

The window slid down; she put her iPhone in one jean pocket, and the solar charger in another. She crawled through the open window and onto the top of the car. She watched as her father and mother struggled to get through their window, before they finally extricated themselves and crawled onto the roof.

She watched in horror as an overhanging limb swept her mother from the top of the car, dragged her husband after her as he frantically tried to hold on to her. They were swept downstream. The limb struck Angie in the middle of her body and she doubled over it. She used the muscles in her arms and legs, strengthened by her conditioning regimen, to work her way back to a notch in the tree where she passed out.

* * *

The storm passed...

Angie heard a voice, and opened her eyes. Where there had been a raging torrent, there was only a shallow creek running by the tree. And a towheaded boy seven or eight years old, squinting as he looked into the sun. Looking at her.

"Lady, what are you doing in at tree?" he asked.

"I can't get down," she said. "Do you see my mom and dad?"

"Nome, they ain't nobody else here but me,

"Do you live around here?"

"Nome. I'm on that wagen train over yonder," he said.

"Wagon train?" *He must be playing.*

"What's your name?"

"Jeremy."

"Jeremy is there anyone at your house that can help me?" she asked.

"I ain't got no house," he said.

"Where do you live?"

"In a wagen. We're going to Orgen."

"Where's your mother?"

"I speck she's cooking supper," the boy said.

"What about your father?"

"My what?" he asked.

"Your dad, father, papa, or whatever you call him."

"I ain't got no pa. They's just Uncle Chester, Aunt Bess, and Ma."

"Do you think you can find someone could help me get down?"

"Yessum. Uncle Chester can. I'll go git him." He ran off, holding on to the floppy hat that had fallen off when he looked up into the tree.

I wonder if he will come back? As high as I am off the ground, I might break something if I try to jump.

Ten minutes later, she saw two men on horseback. The towhead was sitting in front of one of them.

"Jeremy, where is this lady you said needed help?"

"Up air." Jeremy said and pointed to the tree.

"Ma'am, why are you in that tree?" the man with Jeremy asked.

Still in shock, she remained motionless and silent. She was crying but no tears flowed.

"You cain't get back down?"

"I don't think I can without breaking something," she answered. "Can you help me?"

"I reckon we might be able to do something. Let me just think on it for a minute." He dismounted, and walked around examining the situation from several angles.

He took a rope from his saddle and tried to throw one end over her limb. Each try was blocked by the foliage over her head. "Ma'am?"

"Yes?"

"I'm going to throw the rope to you. Ketch it and drop the end across the limb. I'll tie it off and you can kinda shinny down. Try not to come down fast or you'll git blisters on yore hands."

She caught the rope and did as he said. The strength in her arms allowed her to come down hand over hand without sliding. When she was safely on the ground, she said, "That's a relief. Did you see my parents? They were with me. Thank you, Jeremy, for going for help."

"Yessum. I knowed Uncle Chester could do it. He can do just about anything."

"Where's your wagen at?" Chester asked.

"It was washed down the creek during the flood."

"How long were you in the tree?"

"I don't know," she said.

CHAPTER FOUR

The Wagon Train

"Miss, who are you? And where are you from?" the man with Jeremy asked.

"I'm Angela Thornton. I'm from Brevard. Can we look for my parents? They were with me."

"I'm Chester Akins, you've met Jeremy, and this here is Hiram Lewis."

Hiram touched the brim of his hat and said, "Ma'am."

Where is this Breevard?" Chester asked.

"It's close to Independence," she answered.

"What are you doing way out here?"

"I don't remember. I guess I was knocked out, but came to when he...," she pointed to Jeremy, "said something."

"How long have you been out here?"

"I don't know. I don't remember anything after we went into the water."

"We? Who else was with you?"

"My mother and father."

"Where are they?" Hiram Lewis asked.

"I don't know, I think they were swept away. I need to go look for them. I just don't remember anything." She began crying. Real tears.

"I don't see no sign of no storm," Chester said.

"Me neither," Hiram echoed.

"Miss, did you git hit in the head or something?"

"I don't think so," she said. "It doesn't hurt or anything." Her customary ponytail had come undone. She ran her fingers through her hair and found it matted. It felt dirty. "I don't feel any bumps or anything, but it's all tangled."

"Lady, why are you wearing pants?" Jeremy asked.

"It's just something girls my age do," she replied.

"Ain't no girls in our wagon train wears pants," he replied doggedly.

"They might feel better if they did."

"Them's funny shoes."

Jeremy was like a dog playing with a bone. He didn't let go. "They're called sneakers," she replied.

"So you can sneak up on people?"

"Jeremy, don't ask so many questions," Chester said. "Miss Thornton, we'd better get you back to the wagons and let Clint know about this."

"Who is Clint?" she asked.

"He's the wagon master. He's in charge of everything."

"Do you think someone could take me to Brevard? I want to try to find Mom and Dad."

"I tell you ma'am, I don't recollect passing through no place named Breevardm," Chester said. "I know he won't send a wagon back. We're three days out of Independence, and it would be too far to take you back. You can double up with Hiram there and we'll go on back to our train."

"How far is it?" she asked.

"It's less than a mile," Chester said.

"I'll walk then."

"Jeremy, you walk back with her and make sure she don't get lost again."

"Yessir," Jeremy replied. "It ain't far," he told her. He picked up a small stone and threw it at a tree.

"You have a strong arm," she said.

"Yeah. I mean, yes ma'am." he grinned as he said it.

"How old are you," she asked.

"Eight going on nine. How old are you?"

"I'm seventeen going on eighteen."

"You're old. But not as old as Mama or Uncle Chester. They're real old."

I wish my life was as uncomplicated as his. After what has happened, I will never be the same. I don't know what is going on. How long was I in the tree? That Chester guy was right. There isn't any sign of a flood. So what happened to Mom and Dad? Am I dreaming?

She remembered the iPhone in her pocket. When she looked at it, it said 'No Signal'. *So much for that.*

"What's 'at?" Jeremy asked.

She decided not to lie, but to dodge the question. "It's just something my father gave me for Christmas."

"Oh." And the subject was dropped. "There's the train," he said.

Angie looked in the direction he pointed expecting to see the Amtrak California Zephyr. Instead, all she saw was covered wagons. A lot of covered wagons. In a circle.

Oh dear God. What is happening to me? Is this a reenactment?

"Our wagon is right there," Jeremy told her. All of the wagons looked the same to her.

"How can you tell which one is yours?" she asked.

She could tell he thought it was a dumb question because of the expression on his face. "Because that's Mama cooking."

"I should have known that," she said.

"Yeah."

* * *

The wagon train...

"Mama, this is the lady that was in the tree," Jeremy said.

"Mind your manners, Jeremy."

"What happened, dear?"

"We were returning home from Lincoln, and there was a flash flood. My parents were swept away and I wound up in a tree, where Jeremy found me. I'm sure they both drowned, but I didn't see them." she answered, managing to keep her tears at bay.

"Why that's plumb terrible. I am sorry. I'm Hannah Scoggins. I believe you met my brother."

"Yes ma'am. I'm Angela Thornton."

"Were you hurt?"

"My shoulder's sore, but I don't think I'm bleeding or anything."

"Let's get in the wagon, away from all of these prying eyes," Hannah said.

"Your face and neck look fine. Let me see your arms."

Angie's blouse had short sleeves, Mrs. Scoggins raised an eyebrow at what she saw, and then gasped. "Why your arms are all bruised up. It ain't no wonder your shoulder hurts. It's probably bruised up too.

"If you don't mind my saying so, you're dressed funny."

"These are called jeans. My father bought them for me to wear when we travel."

"They look like they're too small for you, but it sure would be nice not to have to worry about these long dresses and petticoats. People would sure talk about me though."

"Do you remember how you got in the tree?"

"The limb that knocked mother in the water hit me in the stomach and the next thing I remember is Jeremy."

* * *

The Wagon master…

"I'm Clint Adams, Miss Thornton. I'm the wagon master of this outfit. Chester here tells me you got caught in a flood."

"Yes sir. It carried my parents away, and I was unlucky enough to get caught up on a tree limb."

"I'd say you were mighty lucky, myself."

"I lost everything. I don't call that lucky. I should have let go and gone with them." Her tears overflowed, streaking her face.

"I haven't seen any sign of a rain myself," he said. In fact, we haven't seen any since we left Independence."

"Feel my shoes," she said. "They're still damp. Look at my hair, and the bruises on my arms. What more do you need?"

"Miss, don't go getting all riled. I'm just telling you we haven't had any rain near us. We weren't no more than twelve or fifteen miles away."

"I don't know what to tell you, Mr. Adams. Either you believe me or you don't. Right now, I just don't care. About anything." She turned and started walking away from the Thornton wagon.

"Where are you going?" he asked.

"I'm going to Brevard to see if I can get some help finding my parents."

"I've been driving wagons on this trail for eight years, and I have never heard of a place called Brevard."

"All right then, I'm going to Independence." She continued walking.

"You're going to die out there," he told her.

"I don't care. I should have died with my parents."

"Miss, you could run into Indians out there," the wagon master said.

"What do you mean?"

"You might run into a raiding or hunting party. Why do you think we are all circled up like this?"

"The Indians have been on the rampage hereabouts since the wagon trains started coming through. There are five different tribes in Nebraska, Wyoming and Montana. None of them like the white man."

His last two sentences fell on deaf ears. Her eyes rolled back in her head as her knees buckled, and she fell to the ground.

"Get some water, Miz Scoggins," the wagon master directed. "Jeremy, see if you can find Jed Lewis. Tell him I'd for him to take someone and look for Miss Thornton's parents."

"Yessir."

CHAPTER FIVE

Angie's Decision

The water from the wet neckerchief on her forehead ran down her face, leaving tracks in the dust on her face. Her eyes fluttered open. "What happened?" she asked.

"You passed out," Hannah Scoggins said. "You must have been hit on the head. How do you feel now?"

"I don't know. Nothing hurts. I've never fainted in my life. I don't understand any of this."

"You lie down in the back of our wagon. I'll bring you some stew in a little while. Keep that cloth on your head. We don't have a doctor in the company. Miz Parnell helps look after anyone that gets sick. She might be able to give you a potion. I sent Jeremy for her after he got back from looking for the Lewis boy."

"Don't do that. I'll be okay in a little while."

"He's already gone. She'll be here in a minute."

Later…

"I'm Ada Parnell. What's your name, dear?"

"Angela Thornton."

"You never had the vapors before?"

"I don't know what that is, but I don't think so."

"Vapors is being dizzy or fainting," Mrs. Parnell said.

"No, I've never done that."

"You don't know how you come to be in that tree?"

"I told them, we were washed away in a flash flood. Both my parents were carried away. I wish I had been instead of getting caught up by that limb."

"Child, there ain't been no rain hereabouts in a long time."

"Then why were my shoes wet?"

"You peed on them."

"I most certainly did not," Angela said, indignantly.

"Ain't no cause to git riled. I'm just trying to hep you."

"No cause? My parents are gone, I don't know where I am and no one believes anything I say. Why wouldn't I be upset? Please, just leave me alone."

Mrs. Parnell climbed out of the wagon. Angela heard her tell the wagon master, "I think she's just addled. Too much sun, maybe."

Angie heard Mrs. Parnell walk away, so she called out, "Mr. Adams, if you're still there, may I talk to you for a minute, please?"

He came to the back of the wagon. "I sent Jed Lewis and Clem looking for your parents. You wanted to talk to me?"

"Yes sir. Thank you for sending someone to look, Mr. Adams. I heard what that lady told you. I am not crazy. I do not know what caused all of this, but I told you the truth. My shoes were wet when Jeremy found me. I have just finished high school and I was a good student. I was born January 27, 1998 in Brevard, Missouri. My parents and I had been to Lincoln, Nebraska to see if I might want to go to college there. It was June 10, 2015. We were returning home when the storm came up. I was in the back seat when Dad lost control of the car and we skidded into the water.

"Why are you looking at me so funny?"

"I think Mrs. Parnell might be right. You said you were born in 1998. Miss Thornton, today is June 10, 1866."

"Mr. Adams, have you ever seen any clothes like mine?"

"No, and I have only seen two or three ladies wearing men's clothes."

"These aren't men's clothes, these are girl's jeans. Look at my shoes. You've never seen anything like them, have you?"

"No." He had a puzzled look on his face. "Can't say as I have."

"That's because they haven't been invented yet. Wait. I just thought of something. I have something I had in my hands when we went in the water. I put it in my pocket before I climbed out of the car. Do you promise not to tell anyone if I show it to you?"

His face reddened. "Now I don't know that I can do that."

"Then I won't show you."

"What is this thing?" he asked.

"It was my Christmas present last year. It is called an iPhone and I promise you've never seen the likes of it, and never will in your lifetime."

"I give you my word. I'll hold it to myself."

She stood as straight as she could within the confines of the wagon, and took her iPhone from her pocket. "This is it. I could listen to music, take pictures, and talk to any other phone in the whole world if I know their number. That part won't work now, but the rest of it will.

"It works off battery power, so I have to be careful with it so I don't run it down. If I did, I might not be able to recharge it if my solar charger was damaged. She touched the Photo icon and pictures displayed. She touched one and it enlarged. These are my parents. You can see our car in the background. This was taken when we were at the college."

She held it up in front of her and touched another icon. There was a click and a flash. The wagon master jumped back. Angie laughed. "It's all right. Look at this."

She held the camera up where he could see it. "I just took this picture of you. What do you think?"

He was stunned. "I saw cameras before, but they put their head under a hood or something and held a little tray above their head. You didn't see the pictures for several days either."

"You see why I asked you not to tell anyone about this?"

"They wouldn't believe it anyways," he said. "I find it hard to believe myself."

"So do I, Mr. Adams, and I'm living it. I've never heard of like this before. I've heard of people saying they were abducted by aliens, but they are crossed off as being crazy, the same as Mrs. Parnell says I am."

"Obviously, you can't go off walking to Independence, for several reasons," Adams said. "One being it's too far, another is I can't send anyone with you. You wouldn't know any more people there than you know here anyhow.

"My suggestion would be to stay with us. You're protected and we have some good people with us."

"I have to do something though. I can't just take charity from people that don't have much to start with."

"I don't suppose you can drive a wagon, so that's out. Miz Gilley is with child and is having a hard time of it. You could maybe help them in exchange for your chuck. I'll talk to them. You might could marry up with one of the unattached men. You are right comely, so I imagine that wouldn't be hard to do."

"Mr. Adams, I'm nowhere near ready to get married. I won't even think about that."

"Like I said, you don't have an awful lot of choices. An unattached woman with no means is not a good thing out here. She doesn't have anyone to protect her."

"Protect from what?"

"Men would be the main thing; the wives would be another."

"Why would I have trouble with wives?"

"They're going to be afraid you might steal their man and leave them in the same situation you find yourself."

"I would never do that," Angie said, as her cheeks turned red at the thought of such a thing.

"They don't know that. You watch, over the next few days, you're going to see what I mean."

"Would you introduce me to the woman who is expecting?"

"I will. I'll also see if I can scare up a change of clothes for you. What you're wearing is not going to help your cause. You might also try to make yourself look as young as possible too."

Later...

"Miss Thompson, Jed and Clem rode several miles downstream and didn't see any signs of your parents or a flood. Miz Gilley said she would be thankful for the help. I'll introduce you. I suggest you not tell them what you told me."

"No sir, but I have a question. What do I tell them when I don't know how to do any of the things they do, like wash clothes, and stuff?"

"Just tell them you were raised in town and your parents had a maid that did those kinds of things. You'll just have to make things up as you go."

"Yes sir. I hate to lie, but I guess I have to stretch the truth. Mom did have a maid."

"Good. Mrs. Craig and Mrs. Whipple offered these two dresses for you."

"Thank you Mr. Adams. Everyone is being so kind. I don't know what to say."

CHAPTER SIX

Angela Meets Jed

"Miz Gilley, this is Angela Thornton. She's going to help you while she's figuring things out." Major Adams said.

"It's nice to meet you, Mrs. Gilley, Mr. Gilley. I appreciate you taking me in. I'll help you all I can. I am an only child so I don't know how much help I'll be."

"I'm sure it's going to be all right," Seth Gilley said, "and I do appreciate whatever you can do to help Polly. We wouldn't have come on this trip if we'd known she was with child."

Polly Gilley was an attractive woman, but she appeared pale and wan. She still greeted Angela with a smile. "It's not your fault, Seth. You couldn't have known I was going to be sick every morning."

"All the same…"

"When is your baby due, Mrs. Gilley?" Angie asked.

"Call me Polly. Mrs. Gilley makes me seem so old. I'm hoping it doesn't come until we get to Oregon. I'd like for him or her to be born in our new home."

Supper was a basic beef stew. "Thank you for the dinner." Angela said, "I'll wash the dishes, Mr. Gilley."

"We don't normally use water, but since the creek is close, we can this time," he replied.

"How would you wash them other times?"

"Scrub them with sand, and rinse the sand off," he told her.

"Oh, so you don't use hot water?"

"That would waste wood that we need to cook."

"I told you I didn't know anything. I'm sorry."

"You'll learn. Just ask."

"Yes sir. I will."

Angie had trouble falling asleep on the hard bed of the wagon. When she realized Mr. Gilley would normally sleep in the wagon with his wife, instead of on the ground beneath on a bedroll, it was too late to change. *I'm not going to put them out any more than I have to. I'll sleep under the wagon tomorrow night.*

The next morning…

Polly was green from the morning sickness and did not eat. "I wish there was something I could do," Angela told her.

"So do I," Polly replied.

When the wagons began rolling, Angela was walking beside the wagon. "Why don't you ride while you can?" Seth asked.

"It wouldn't be right. I'm okay. I'm used to a lot of exercise," Angela answered. "No faster than we're moving, I won't have any trouble keeping up."

"They can hold this pace all day," he told her.

"Mr. Gilley, I can do whatever I have to, I'm in good physical condition."

"I'm sure you'll do all right with us. I'm glad you're here."

When the noon break was called, she tried to help Polly with lunch, but Polly told her to rest. She was leaning back against a wheel when Jeremy came up. "Ah, here's my rescuer," she said. "Good morning, Jeremy.

"Are you gonna go to Orgen with us?"

"You mean Or-re-gon."

"That's what I said. Orgen."

I don't know what I'm going to do," she answered.

"At man asked me your name."

"What man?" she asked.

"Jed. On the next wagen."

"Did you tell him?"

"Yes ma'am."

"You don't have to say ma'am to me."

"Yes ma'am I do. I'll get a whupping if'n I don't."

"Where's your wagon?"

"In front of Jed Lewis's."

"We're starting up. Hadn't you better go back to your wagon?"

"Nome. Mama knows where I am."

"Don't you ride in the wagon?"

"Some. But I like to walk. Mama just whistled. Guess I better go afore she gets riled at me."

"Tell your mother I said hello and thanks again."

"Yessum, I will." He ran toward his wagon.

Angela heard him say, "Hey Jed, I tole her your name," as he passed the Lewis wagon.

That evening…

She had scrubbed the metal plates with sand and rinsed them as she had been directed when he walked up.

"Jeremy told me your name is Miss Thornton," he said. "I'm Jedadiah Lewis, but folks call me Jed."

"I'm pleased to meet you, Jed. I'm Angela, but I prefer Angie."

"You're the one Pa helped out of the tree."

"Guilty as charged. Before you ask, I still don't know how I got there."

"Papa told us."

A pretty girl walked up. "Jed, introduce me to your friend."

His face flushed. "She's not my friend. I mean I just met her. Angela Thornton, this is my sister, Mandy. Be careful around her. She's mean."

"Why Jedadiah Alan Lewis. That's a terrible thing to say about your older sister. It's nice to meet you, Angie.

I'm glad you're joining up with us. It will be nice to have someone around to talk to that has some sense. You can run along now, Jed."

"I'm going snake hunting," he said. "If I can find one, I'm going to put a rattler in your bedroll."

"If you ever saw a rattler, it would light a shuck under your tail, and you'd hightail it out of there."

"I better mosey on out of here before I get in trouble. Papa told me I have to quit hitting you. It was nice meeting you Angie."

"You too," Angie said.

After he left, she asked, "Do you two go at it all the time?"

"No, only when other people are around. He's a nice brother. He would die protecting me if he had to," Mandy said.

"I am… was an only child. I always wished I had a sister, I would have someone to talk to," Angie said. "Mom was my best friend, but there were just some things I would rather not discuss with her."

"I wish I had a sister too, but not if I had to give up my brother."

"Does he have a girlfriend?"

Mandy laughed. "Yep, his horse.

"I had a boyfriend back in Steubenville. If we had stayed there, I guess Calvin and I would have eventually married."

"Did you love him?" Angie asked.

"I liked him, but was he *the* one? I don't think so. Mama didn't like him. What about you?"

"I didn't have anyone special," Angie replied. "I didn't even go to the prom."

"What's a prom?"

"It's a fancy dress up dance."

"I never heard of it. In Steubenville, the church had dances once a month during the summer, but they weren't dress up," Mandy said.

"Did you know the Gilley's before?"

"No, they joined up with us in Greenfield."

"Where's that?" Angie asked.

"It's in Indiana. We stopped over there four days. I was ready to stop, too. Poor Jed was really ready. Papa always walked the entire day, and Jed did too until he got sick. He was sick for two days and I had to give up my spot in the wagon and walk during that time."

"I had better go check with Polly," Angie said. "I don't want to slack off. They've been really nice to me."

"I'll see you in the morning. This has been fun. Goodnight, Mandy."

"Night, Angie."

CHAPTER SEVEN

What's She Like?

"You sure talked to her a long time," Jed said to Mandy.

"I guess I did. She's the first girl close to my age since we left home."

"What's she like?"

"I like her. I don't think she's been around much, though. She didn't have a boyfriend where she lived. I think we're going to be good friends."

"I'd like to be her friend. She's pretty," he said.

"Too pretty for you, that's for sure."

"You're probably right. There are several she could choose from if she's of a mind."

"Take some advice from your sister," Mandy said. "Talk to her. Girls like boys to hold up their end of the talking."

"The only thing I know to talk about is farming. She wouldn't be interested in planting wheat."

"Jed, girls like it when boys say nice things about them; things like how they look, their pretty eyes, or hair. You know, we like compliments."

"Did Calvin do that?"

"No, and you notice we didn't get married either. He was nice, but he was boring."

* * *

"Would you like some company this morning?" Mandy asked.

"I'd love some," Angie replied. "Are you sure you wouldn't rather be riding?"

"Maybe later. How's Mrs. Gilley?"

Angie's face clouded. "She's still not doing too well. She couldn't hold anything down again this morning. She really should see a doctor."

"I don't think there will be one in Fort Kearney. Mr. Adams told Papa it isn't a very big place, and we're nearly two months to Fort Laramie. Mrs. Parnell is the closest thing we have, and about the only thing she'll do is give her an aciphidity bag like she gave Jed when he was sick. Honestly, that is the worst smelling stuff you will ever smell."

"What's it for?"

"It's supposed to keep diseases away."

"Does it work?"

"He got well, and he still wears it. You can smell it if you get close to him."

"Mandy, this is embarrassing, but I'm going to ask anyway. Mr. Gilley told me we have to save water. How do you take a bath?"

"You can only do it when we camp next to a creek or river. It's pretty cold too."

"You just go out there and take your clothes off and get in a creek?"

"If you want to take a bath you do. When I do, Jed watches out and makes sure no one gets close. Mama and I both take one at the same time. By the time we get around to it, we smell pretty strong. Some people bathe with their clothes on so they get washed at the same time. Others just don't bother most of the time."

"That's going to take some getting used to," Angie said.

"What are you used to?"

"Everyday."

"That sounds like a big waste of water," Mandy replied. "You won't be able to do that here or where we're going."

"Jeremy says they're going to Oregon. Is that where you're going too?"

"Papa says we're going to start out in Oregon City, but doesn't know where we'll wind up. Where are you going?"

"I don't know where I'm going or what I'm going to do when I get there. I'll have to find some kind of work, but I don't know what it would be. The only thing I've ever done was work in a department store one summer. I doubt there's much call for that now."

"You'll figure it out, and I'll help," Mandy told her.

Angie felt the kindness in Mandy's voice. "You're sweet, Mandy. I'm glad you're my friend."

"Same here. By the way, my idiot brother asked a lot of questions about you last night."

"What kind of questions?"

"What were you like? If you had any boyfriends, those types of questions. He thinks you're pretty."

"What did you tell him?"

"That you were too pretty for him."

"You didn't!"

"Yes, I did. I love him, but I love to tease him too."

"You're mean!" Angie said.

"Yes, but in a nice way, and only to him, and only when I'm teasing."

"How old is he?"

"He'll be eighteen next month. He's a year and a half younger than I am."

"I'll be eighteen in January."

"You're just the right age for him," Mandy said.

"Don't go matchmaking on me now. I'm too young to be married."

"Where we come from, if you're not married by the time you're twenty, you're behind everyone else. You're a spinster if you don't have a husband by twenty-five."

Jed wandered over from his usual place behind their livestock. "Howdy. You're looking nice today," he said to Angie.

"Ignore it and maybe it will go away," Mandy said.

"I wasn't talking to you," he said.

"I knew that right off," she replied. "You've never, ever told me I look nice."

"That should tell you something right there," he replied.

"I do think he can hold his own, Mandy. He got you there."

"Even a blind hog can root around and find an acorn once in a while," Mandy said.

"I'm fine, Jed. How are you?"

"Tired of walking. I'm glad we only have another eighteen hundred miles to go."

"Is there a layover in Fort Kearney?" Angie asked.

"Maybe a couple of days. I doubt it would be much longer," he answered.

"I have a feeling I will be left there," she said.

"That's not going to happen unless it's what you want," Mandy said.

Fort Kearney…

Major Adams declared a two day layover for his caravan.

Seth went in search of a doctor to look at Polly, who was showing no sign of improvement. "Sir, our doctor was transferred to Fort Laramie when the Indians started acting up," the captain told him. "Why do you need a doctor?"

"My wife is with child, and she's been puny for some time. I'm worried about her."

"There's a lady here that's done some midwifing, you might have her take a look. Other than that, I'm afraid your best bet will be Fort Laramie."

The midwife…

After a rudimentary examination, the midwife asked, "Mr. Gilley, other than losing her breakfast, does your wife hurt or anything?"

"She hasn't said anything, but then Polly isn't the complaining type. Do you have any idea what's wrong?"

"No sir. A lot of women get sick of a morning, but they usually get over it by three months. The only thing I can tell you is keep trying to get her to eat something. Doc Turner in Fort Laramie is a good man. He might be able to help. I just wish there was something I could give her, but I don't know of anything that works."

"I thank you, Mrs. Sharp. I reckon we'll just have to keep going."

CHAPTER EIGHT

Fort Laramie

Five weeks later…

July 18, 1866, Fort Laramie, Wyoming Territory

"Doctor Turner, I hope you can help her. She's been sick since we left Independence."

"I'll examine her, but I have a lot more experience with arrows and gunshot wounds than I do with babies. This is my wife, Cora. She'll be in the room while I'm with your wife. If you'll wait in the hall, please."

Seth looked up to see Angela approaching. "You didn't have to come," he said.

"I wanted to be here," she told him. "I hope he can find out what's wrong with her. I feel so sorry for her when she's sick. She's almost afraid to eat at all, and I can't blame her. Are you going to go on with the train?"

"It depends on what the doctor says. If we can't go now, and she gets better, we might be able to get with another one later. It can't be too much later because

Major Adams told me you have to get through the mountains before the first snow.

"What will you do if the doctor tells us not to travel?" he asked.

"I don't know. Everything is day to day with me. I just don't know what's waiting around the next bend."

"If we have to stay, you can stay with us and keep doing what you are now. Polly told me she couldn't make it without you."

"That's kind of her to say. I feel like I'm such a burden."

The Doctor…

Dr. Turner, Angela here, has been helping Polly."

"Hello, Angela, it's nice to meet you. My wife, Cora.

"Mr. Gilley, I didn't find anything physically wrong with your wife. I think it is a case of extended morning sickness. It is not unknown for it to last all the way to delivery. Before you ask, there is nothing known to give relief.

"Are you sick all day long?" he asked Polly.

"No sir, most of the time it gets better by lunch, but not always. It's worse in the morning," Polly answered.

"Should we stop and wait until after the baby comes?" Seth asked.

"You might be a little more comfortable out of the wagon, but I can't say it would help otherwise. I would suggest rather than eating first thing in the morning you hold off till later in the day. It's always been my opinion the nausea is triggered by the aroma of frying food, such as bacon. It might help, then again, it might not."

"If we decide to stay, would there be a house we could rent or something?"

"There might, but I have to tell you, Fort Laramie is expensive. I hate to say it, but the store keepers take advantage of the situation. Believe it or not, they have two sets of prices. One for the settlers and the other set for those that live here. It isn't right, but it's the way it is. I couldn't afford to live here if the Army didn't provide me with quarters."

"Seth, I think I could fix breakfast, if that would help," Angie said. "I can't do biscuits, but maybe I could do some of it. I'd like to try. I owe you two so much."

Later…

"Mandy, can you cook?"

"Some. I'm not as good as Mama, but I wouldn't starve if I had to live off what I can cook."

"Can you teach me? The doctor thinks the fried food smell might be what's upsetting Polly. I want to do something to help."

"I'll do what I can, Mama would be better."

"I don't want to impose on your mother. She has enough to take care of without me bothering her. Don't say anything, I shouldn't have asked about it. I need to go check on Polly."

"You're as bad as Jed. There's nothing wrong in asking a friend for help."

"It's just that… I hate to bother people, especially when I have nothing to offer in return."

"That sounds a lot like you're feeling sorry for yourself," Mandy said.

"I guess I'm guilty of that too. Can you imagine losing all of your family and finding yourself in the middle of a bunch of strangers with nothing but the clothes you're wearing?"

"I can't, and I hope I never have to experience it either."

"No one should," Angela said.

"Have you ever eaten mush?"

"No. I can't say I have."

"It's easy to fix. It's something we have often for breakfast. All you do is boil water, add some cornmeal and a little salt and butter if you have it. Of course you have to use the right amount of corn meal as well as water."

"Mother used to tell people I couldn't boil water without scorching it," Angie said.

"She sounds like fun."

"She was. She was also my best friend."

Later…

"Mama told me to give you this. It's her receipt for mush."

"It looks easy enough. What are currants?"

Mandy described them as being dried grapes. "Oh, you mean raisins."

"I never heard of those, but I would bet Mrs. Gilley has some."

"Why yes, I believe I have some left," Polly said. I use them in mush frequently."

Angie grinned. "I asked Mandy Lewis if she could help me learn a little about cooking so I could make it easier on you. She brought me a recipe for it." She showed the paper to Polly.

"That's the way I make it. It's quick and easy. I'll show you how in the morning."

"I'm trying to keep you away from having to do any of that."

"I don't know whether mush would bother me or not. I also fry the leftovers some times, and have them for breakfast."

The North Platte River Crossing…

The wagons with oxen were ferried across the raging North Platte River, taking two wagons each trip. The pole man was trying mightily to keep the raft straight while the other men pulled for the other shore using the cable. The first ten wagons crossed safely. The Lewis and Gilley wagons were two thirds of the way across when the wind and shifting currents caused one of the oxen to momentarily lose its balance and stumble. The raft tilted steeply to the left. Mandy was standing with Angela alongside the wagons. When the raft tilted, Mandy fell into the water and was being pushed downstream by the swift current. She screamed and with arms flailing, went beneath the surface.

With no hesitation, Angela dove in after her. The cold water was a shock, but with strong, swift strokes, she caught up with the struggling Mandy. Her wildly swinging arms made it difficult for Angie to grab her and she disappeared under the surface again. The muddy water obscured any vision Angie might have had. She swung her arms back and forth in the cold water.

There! She felt fabric and grabbed hold and kicked her way to the surface. Mandy was still struggling. "Don't fight me, Mandy. I know what I'm doing."

In a harsh voice she said, "If you keep fighting me, we're both going to die. Just relax. I'm going to flip you onto your back. Then I'm going to put my arm over your chest and get us to the bank. I can do this, but only if you calm down. Okay? Let's do it." She began kicking her strong legs and pulling for the riverbank.

CHAPTER NINE

Rescued

Men from the wagons already across, ran down river to the girls. When they neared the bank one of the men threw a rope. Angie managed to get it around Mandy's chest and the men hauled her to the bank. They pulled her from the cold water. Another pulled Angie to the bank by grabbing her hand.

"Put her face down on the ground," she directed.

She turned Mandy's head to the side, resting on one arm. Forcing her mouth open, Angie put her finger in Mandy's mouth and moved it around. She straddled the still body, and placed her hands on Mandy's back, thumbs along the spine and began compressions. Water spewed from the prone girl's mouth and she began coughing.

The Lewis's wagon and livestock made it to the far bank. Hiram, Sophie, and Jed ran to join the crowd. After glancing at the two shivering, soaked girls,

Sophie said, "Get them back to the wagon. They're freezing."

Hiram picked up Mandy while Jed carried Angie back to the train and placed them in the back of the wagon. Sophie put the flap down, closing off the rear of the wagon, and began helping them remove their wet clothes. Leaving their underwear, she pushed the rest through the flap and directed Jed to hang them out to dry. She wrapped the girls with buffalo robes they had purchased in Fort Laramie.

"Jed, find another dress for Angela," Sophie directed. "Get a fire started and move her clothes close so they'll dry faster.

"There's no way we can ever repay you for what you did. Since you no longer have a family of your own, from now on, you are a part of ours."

That brought tears to Angie's eyes. "Thank you," she said. "That means a lot to me."

"Mama, you can't do that," Mandy said. "It would crush Jed. He's sweet on her, and a boy can't be sweet on his sister. At least not the way he is."

Her mother smiled, and said, "So that's what it is. I thought he was cow eyed over something. It's Angela."

"You two are crazy, Angie replied.

"The highlight of his life was carrying you back to the wagon," Mandy told her.

Changing the subject, Angie said, "I guess we've had our bath, haven't we?"

"I may never go near the water again," Mandy declared. "I have never seen anyone, man or boy swim like you did."

"I practically lived in the water when I was a little girl. I had better go help Polly. I wonder if my clothes are close to being dry."

"I'll check for you," Sophie said. She returned carrying the clothes. "Here you are, nice and warm, although they may be a bit damp in places."

"They're fine." Angie got dressed and left the wagon.

"That was incredible," Mandy told her mother. "She was so calm. She told me if I didn't stop struggling, we were both going to die there. She said she knew what she was doing. And she really did."

"You should have seen it from our end. She was in the water and after you in the blink of an eye. No one else had moved. I thought we had lost you." She hugged her daughter. "We were truly blessed when she joined up with our company."

"I wonder where she learned it." Mandy asked.

"It doesn't matter. She was here when we needed her," her mother replied.

The Gilley wagon…

"Seth told me what you did," Polly said to Angela. "That was brave of you."

"She was in trouble," Angie dismissed the praise.

"You risked your life to try to save another person. Not many would do that."

"I had nothing to lose."

"Losing your life is a lot more than nothing."

"I wish…" She couldn't finish the sentence.

"Think about this. If you had died when your parents did, that girl you rescued this morning would be dead right now. It's because of you she's still alive. That's the greatest gift you can give anyone."

"I could not do anything to help when the two people most important to me needed me. I can't get past that," Angie said.

Later…

"Good morning, sister," Mandy said, when she joined Angie after the wagons began moving.

Angie's cheeks flushed at the affectionate greeting. "Good morning yourself. How are you doing this morning?"

"I'm okay," Mandy said. "Thanks to you."

"You would have done the same for me."

"We would both have drowned if that had been the case. Mama said you were the only one that did anything on the raft. I would not be here if it weren't for you."

"I'm glad it worked out for both of us. Let's not make a big deal of it."

It is a big deal," Mandy said. "No one in our family will ever forget it."

"Where's Jed this morning?"

"He went out with the scout to see if there's any sign of Indians, and to look for camping places. I think they'll be out a couple of days. Why?"

"I was just curious, that's all."

CHAPTER TEN

Angie and Jed

The train had made camp for the evening when Jed and the scout rejoined them. He was grubby and dusty when he removed the saddle and bridle and turned his horse to graze in the corral formed by the circled wagons. He slapped his hat against his leg to shake off some of the dust.

He spied Angela by the cooking pit next to the Lewis wagon and approached her. "I didn't do a proper job of thanking you for what you did for Mandy. She's not worth much, but she's the only sister I have, and I appreciate it."

"I'm glad I was there," she said.

"I was swimming my horse and the stock across and didn't know what happened until I was up on the far bank and it was over. I'm not much of a swimmer, but I would have tried if I'd known."

"Mandy's been a good friend to me and Lord knows I don't have many of them anymore."

"I would like to be your friend," he said, his head lowered from the embarrassing admission.

"I would like to have you as a friend," she told him.

"What are you two in a deep conversation about?" Mandy asked. "My nose itches, so you must be talking about me."

"You have a lot of nose to itch," he said. "I was just thanking her for the other day."

"Where were you when it happened?" Mandy asked.

"I was downstream with the stock, and didn't know anything about it until it was over."

"You need to go down to the creek and jump in, clothes and all," his sister told him. "You smell horsey."

"After two days in the saddle, you'd smell horsey yourself."

"Don't you two ever let up?" Angie asked.

"Not very often," Mandy admitted. "He'd think I didn't love him if I wasn't on him."

"I'd never think anything like that, Sis," he said and draped his arm around her shoulder.

"I envy both of you having each other."

"You shouldn't. You have both of us now," Mandy told her.

"Amen to that," Jed said. "I wonder if I have time to go to the creek before Mama has supper ready."

"You go and I'll ask her to hold off a few minutes."

"Can you eat with us, Angie?" he asked.

"I wouldn't want to surprise your mother unexpectedly."

"I'll ask her," Mandy said. "She can always add some water to the stew."

Dinner around the campfire…

"How was your trip with the scout?" Hiram asked his son.

"It was great. We saw a large herd of buffalo. I think a hunting party is going to go out and try to get a couple for meat. Slade pointed out some Indian sign, but we never saw any. He saw things I didn't see until he pointed them out.

"We also found three places with good grass and water. We'll be camping at those for the next two or three days. We hobbled the horses at night so they wouldn't wander off.

What's been going on around here?"

"Nothing. Same old thing," Mandy said. "Walk, stop. And walk some more. One of the boys from another wagon came over and walked with us. He never looked at me once. He only had eyes for Angie."

Angie's eyes widened at the blatant falsehood. She started to say something, but Mandy shook her head the slightest amount.

When they were alone she asked, "Why did you say that? It wasn't true and you know it."

"I was just trying to stir the pot a little," Mandy confessed.

"Are you trying to play matchmaker between Jed and me? If you are, stop it. I don't need a boyfriend let alone a husband."

"You never know what's in store for tomorrow."

"You don't have a boyfriend," Angie pointed out.

"I had one. You said you never have. You could do a lot worse than Jed."

"I should have let you drown."

"At least you show a little spirit once in a while. Maybe there's hope for you yet."

Later…

"Angie, do you feel like taking a walk?" Jed asked.

"I've walked all day. It's the last thing I feel like."

"You're right. I didn't think. I'm sorry." He turned and walked away.

The plaintive note in his voice touched a tender spot. "Jed, wait. As long as we don't walk too far, I'll be okay."

"It's a nice cool evening," he said, I thought you might enjoy it."

"What Mandy said wasn't true about someone walking with us."

"Oh I know that. She was just trying to get me riled," he told her.

"I can't walk any more. My feet are really sore."

"Can we sit for a minute?"

"That would be a relief," she replied.

"You sit there," he said, and sat opposite her. "Take off your shoe."

"What is this, some kind of a joke?"

"No joke, seriously."

She removed her shoe. He took her foot across his leg and began massaging it. She sighed, "That feels good."

He removed the other shoe and did the same thing with the other foot. "There you go. Does that feel better?"

"It does. Where did you learn that?"

"Right after we left Steubenville, one of the men on the train told me about it. His wife got sick and they turned around and went back to Steubenville, but I remembered about the foot rub. He said his wife did his every evening."

"It felt good. Jed, I want to be your friend, but I really don't want a boyfriend."

"That's okay. I can use a friend."

"Mandy is your friend too."

"I know that, but she's my sister and is supposed to be. Ready to go back?"

"Did you enjoy your walk in the moonlight?" Mandy asked.

"It was very refreshing," Angie said. "I'm going to check to see if I can do anything for Polly."

After she left, Jed said, "Mandy, she really has a problem. Her shoes are worn thin as paper. In a few days, they will be worn through to her socks."

"I'm not even going to ask how you found that out."

"We only walked a little ways and she begged off because her feet hurt. I asked her to sit, and gave her a foot rub. That's how I know. We have to do something."

"I'll talk to Mama. She can probably repair them."

When Mandy asked, her mother said, "I can probably do something to them that will help."

* * *

"Angie, I can probably do something about your shoes if you'd like," Sophie said.

"Why is everyone so concerned about my shoes all of a sudden?"

"Because we love you," Sophie said.

"Now look what you've gone and done," Angie said as her eyes filled with tears.

"I have leather and needles I use to repair Jed and Hiram's; now with Mandy walking more, I'll probably have to do hers too."

"I doubt you've seen shoes like mine. They're not very common."

"You're right, but I'm pretty resourceful, I can keep you from walking on bare ground."

"I appreciate it, Mrs. Lewis."

CHAPTER ELEVEN

A Change of Heart

The caravan made camp early because of the good water and grass. "Are you too tired to take a short walk?" Jed asked Angie. The walk took them to the creek. "Is it hard for you when you see a creek like this?"

"Sometimes I get flashbacks, and it makes me remember what happened."

"Yet you went in the water after Mandy."

"If I had taken time to think about it, I might not have done it."

"It's the bravest thing I've ever seen. If I had been there, I would have tried, and probably drowned in the attempt. I'm not even in your class as a swimmer."

She changed the subject. "You're sneaky, you know that? So is your sister."

"Why are you calling us sneaky?" Jed asked.

"Because you told your mother about my shoes being worn."

"Would you have said anything?"

She hung her head. "No."

"Somebody had to say something. The bottoms would have worn through in a couple of days. You probably dismiss me as some kind of dull witted farmer. Actually, I always did well in school."

"What did you do back in Ohio?" she asked.

"We had a nice farm in Steubenville and did pretty well with it."

"Why did you leave?" she asked.

"Papa was in the war, and was lucky enough to come back. A lot of our neighbors didn't and their families were hurting. I was twelve when he left, but Mama, Mandy and I were able to grow enough to feed us and pay the taxes. That's all we needed. When Papa came back, nobody had the money to buy anything.

"Our farm had a big seam of coal on it. We were right on the Ohio River so shipping it would be cheap, and the Steubenville Coal Mining Company wanted it enough to pay a big price. Papa decided to take it before they went to some of the neighbors with an offer. He signed up with Major Adams, and got our rig together and here we are. When we get to Oregon, we'll be able to claim more land free than we had in Ohio. I'll be able to file a claim on my own. It was a good opportunity for us to start over.

"What about Mandy? She had a boyfriend. It must have been hard for her to leave."

"You know how she is, she likes everyone. Her boyfriend's main interest was our farm. His family was trash. Mama and Papa knew it, but Mandy didn't. She thinks everybody is good. They offered to let her stay with Mama's sister, but she didn't want to do that.

"That's enough about the Lewis family. What about yours?"

"Well, I grew up on a large dairy farm in Brevard, Missouri, near Independence. I was a tomboy."

"What's a tomboy?" he asked.

"I liked to climb trees, ride. I get dirty like a boy does. Things most girls don't like."

"What about your parents?"

"They were both great. I think Dad was hoping for a boy and that's why I turned out the way I did. I was definitely a daddy's girl, but when I got hurt, it was Mom I turned to for hugging."

"Living on a dairy farm, you have probably done some milking, Mandy never would try that."

"I know how to milk, but most of ours was done by the milking machines."

"What's a milking machine?" Jed asked.

Realizing she had made a major slip, she decided not to lie. "Jed, if I tell you a personal secret, can you keep it to yourself?"

"I guess," he replied.

"That's not good enough. I'm sorry." She returned to camp, leaving a puzzled eighteen year old sitting on the bank of Plum Creek, wondering what had just happened.

He jumped up and ran after her. "Angie, wait. I can keep your secret."

"I can't take the chance, Jed." She continued walking to the Gilley wagon.

"Angie, please wait. Talk to me."

"I've said too much," she told him. "Just leave me alone please."

The next morning…

"What did you do to my brother?" Mandy demanded.

"I didn't do anything. I just asked him to leave me alone."

"He's like a puppy someone just kicked. What did you say to him?"

"I simply asked him to leave me alone."

"There's more to it than that," Mandy persisted. "I want to know what happened."

"Nothing happened. Will you please let it go?"

"No, I won't let it go. He's my brother, and you hurt him. I don't like it."

Mandy put her hands on Angie's shoulders. "Angie, what in the world is wrong with you?"

"There's nothing wrong with me. I just want to be left alone." She ducked between two wagons to the opposite side. Mandy walked back and climbed into their wagon. They honored Angie's request to be left alone.

* * *

Clint Adams called for a meeting…

"Folks, the reason I called for this meeting is we've got a decision to make. In two days, we're coming to a fork called the Parting of the Ways. The right fork is the Sublette Cutoff. If we take the Sublette Cutoff, it saves us about 85 miles and seven days. You pay a price for this savings though. It is desert, has no water, no wood, and very little grass for forty-five miles. That's hard going for man and beast.

"Instead of that, there's the Slate-Kinney Cutoff that saves forty miles instead of eighty-five, and it cuts the desert crossing to ten miles. It's steeper and rougher.

"You folks are the boss, and I'll go the way you want. I favor the Sublette because of the seven day savings. You'll have to make your water, and wood last."

When the caravan arrived at the fork, ten of the wagons opted for the longer trail. The Gilley's and the Lewis's decided to take the cutoff with the rest of the caravan.

The third day on the cutoff, Mandy saw Angie staggering as she walked beside the wagon. Then she fell. "Papa, Seth, help. Angie fainted."

They stopped the two wagons and ran to where Mandy kneeled by the still girl. Sophie and Polly joined them. "Move her into the shade," she said. "Mandy, get me a wet cloth. She's hot. Seth how's your water holding out?"

"I'll look." He came back. "We have plenty. A lot more than I thought."

"Her lips are parched, and her tongue is swollen. Do you know if she's had any water?" Sophie asked.

"I haven't noticed it while we were moving," Mandy said. She placed the saturated cloth on Angie's forehead. "She hasn't been wearing a bonnet either."

Sophie took the dipper of water from Polly and let a small stream flow onto Angie's lips. She began to stir. "Take a small sip. Don't try to take too much at a time."

Clint Adams had ridden back to see what the holdup was. "What happened?"

"She fainted. I don't think she's been drinking any water," Sophie told him.

"Get her into a wagon and let's get moving. Every minute we stop makes it harder to get started again."

"I wondered why we weren't using more water," Polly said. "Put her in our wagon. I'll keep an eye on her and make sure she takes water."

"She's smarter than that," Sophie said.

"I told them we had to save water after the meeting the other day," Seth said.

"The problem is, she thinks she's a burden on everyone, and is going out of her way not to be," Mandy said.

"We're just going to have to convince her she isn't. She's been a big help to me," Polly said.

CHAPTER TWELVE

Out of the Desert

"We're going to be stopping at Green River tomorrow," Jed told his family, dismounting and dusty from his scouting trip with Slade. The grass is good and so is the water. I think the major is planning a layover, but I don't know how long.

"What's been going on around here?"

"You mean beside Angie passing out from no water and the heat?" Mandy replied.

"Is she all right?"

"Mama can tell you better than I can. She's been helping Polly take care of her."

"Did they run out of water? Couldn't we have given her some of ours?"

"They didn't run out. In fact, they had plenty because she wasn't drinking any. The idiot was trying to save it. She also wasn't wearing a bonnet. I've never seen her wear one. I'll bet she doesn't even have one, and she would never ask to borrow one."

"Do you think it would be all right if I visited her?" he asked."

"I'm sure it would. Especially if you tell her we're stopping tomorrow."

The Gilley wagon…

"Miss Polly, would it be okay if I say hello to Angie?"

She called out, "Angie, Jed Lewis is here and would like to say hello."

"I'll be out in a minute," Angie said.

He stood at the rear of the wagon, hand extended to help her down. She took it and hopped lightly to the ground. "I've been out several days and wanted to say hello and see how you are doing. Mandy told me what happened."

"That was so embarrassing. I know better than that, but I was trying to save water."

"You don't have to worry about that anymore. We're almost out of the desert and will be stopping at Green River tomorrow. I don't know how long the major is planning to lay over."

"That is good news. I'm sure everyone will be relieved to hear it."

"Back on the farm I've stayed in the sun until I was light headed. It's not a good feeling. Are you still feeling the effects?"

"I think I'll be back to walking tomorrow. Thanks for stopping by. It was sweet of you."

"Well, take care, and wear a bonnet. The sun can be a killer."

Angie watched him walk back to the next wagon and begin talking to Mandy.

* * *

The next morning…

The plates had been scrubbed and rinsed. Everything was stowed in preparation for the move out call. Mandy came up to Angie and handed her the bonnet she was carrying. "Jed said you were walking this morning. You need to wear one of these."

"You don't have to do this," Angie said.

"I know I don't, but I want you to have it."

"I'm sorry for the way I acted the other day. I was a real bi… very rude," Angie told her.

"I had no right to say what I said. I'm overly protective of my baby brother."

"Some baby," Angie said, chuckling. "Will you walk with me this morning? I don't know how long I'm going to be able to go, and I'd like to have someone handy to catch me if I fall."

"I'm good to go," Mandy said.

The signal came down the line and the broad line of wagons began moving. "What happened the other day was…"

"You don't have to explain," Mandy told her.

"What happened was, I asked Jed if I told him something could he keep it a secret. He said he didn't know, so I told him I couldn't tell him. He changed and said he could, but at that point, I couldn't trust that he could do it. He persisted, and finally I told him to leave me alone. You came along and I said the same thing to you. That's all it was. A big to-do about nothing, but it cost me a friend."

"If you're talking about me, I'm still your friend, and you don't have to tell me anything."

Angie stopped walking and the two girls hugged, holding each other tightly long enough for the line of wagons to pass. When they broke apart and began to hurry to catch up, Angie said, "Only the major knows this…"

"Angie don't."

"Are you always this bossy? Anyway, I want to tell you and I trust you not to tell anyone. This is the way it was…"

* * *

CHAPTER THIRTEEN

Angie's Story

"This is going to be hard to believe," Angie said. "I don't even believe it myself and I'm living it.

"Mom, Dad and I had been to Lincoln just like I told everyone. It wasn't in a wagon. We were in a car instead."

"There were no railroad tracks anywhere near there," Mandy interrupted.

"Let me go on, and I'll explain all of it that I understand, okay? There was a flash flood and the water was washing across the road. Dad hit the water and lost control of the car and we went into the overflowing creek. I guess I had better explain what a car is. It's metal and is driven by a gasoline engine. They can travel really fast. The desert we're crossing? We could do it in less than an hour in a car." She smiled at the look of incredulity on Mandy's face. "You ain't heard nothing yet.

"Back to the story. We were in the car and going downstream with the flow. I got out through the back window and crawled to the top. My father was trying to get Mom out. We went by a tree, they were swept into the water, and I was caught up in the limbs of the tree. The tree where Jeremy found me."

"I don't understand any of this," Mandy said.

"What year is this?"

Why it's 1866 of course."

"I was born January 27, 1998," Angie said.

"That's impossible. That's what one hundred-twenty years in the future," Mandy said.

"Actually, it's one hundred-thirty-two years. I told you it was hard to believe. I'm going to show you something I've only shown Major Adams and it was to convince him I was telling the truth.

She pulled her phone and the solar charger from her pockets. "This is called an iPhone, and this gadget uses the sun to recharge the battery. You've never seen one because they won't be invented for another one hundred and forty years."

She tapped an icon and the phone came to life. She tapped more icons. "This is my mother and father, and our farm. That is the Lexus we were in when we went into the water." She swiped the screen. "Recognize him?"

"That's Major Adams. And you."

Angie put her arm around Mandy and held the iPhone out in front of them and took a selfie. Mandy heard a click and blinked at the simultaneous flash. "Now look."

"Oh my God," Mandy said.

"It's also a telephone, but phones haven't been invented yet either."

"What were you doing out in the middle of nowhere?"

"It wasn't the middle of nowhere then. It was a little over two hundred miles. About a three and one-half hours' drive. I was an athlete. Do they have baseball now?" Angie asked.

"Yes, I've never seen it, but I've heard of it."

"People that play sports are athletes. I played volleyball and basketball. I was good at both. Several colleges offered me scholarships where they would pay for everything just so I would play for their school. We had been to the University of Nebraska to see if I wanted to go there. I also was on my high school swim team. During the past two summers I was a lifeguard at the municipal swimming pool. That's how I was able to get to you when you fell in the river. Remember, I told you I knew what I was doing? That's how I knew."

"This is so much to take in," Mandy said. "So maybe you were sent to save my life, otherwise I wouldn't be here."

"I never thought of it that way, but I guess it's a possibility, if you believe in divine intervention."

"Are you… are you an angel?"

"I don't think so. I don't think angels faint the way I did the other day."

"So you don't know what happened to your folks, do you?"

"No, but I don't see how they could have survived."

"What if they wound up in another time just like you did? Or just bumped into something and made it to solid ground."

"That's the really hard part. I'll probably never know."

"I'm glad you told me. You don't think you'll be able to go back do you?" Mandy asked.

"No. I would have had a much more comfortable life than walking to Oregon, not knowing how I'm going to get by or anything like that. Back home, I could have gone to college and become a lawyer or a doctor, or anything I wanted to be. Mother and Dad both went. Mom was a teacher. Dad was happy being a dairy farmer.

"Remember when we were talking and I asked you about taking a bath? I did take one every day. We had a gas hot water heater, and I could stand under a hot shower for half an hour and still not run out. As an athlete, I perspired a lot. We had dishwashers and washers and dryers for our clothes.

"It was not all sweet and lovely. Since there were a lot more people, there's a lot more crime. Everyone is always in a big hurry.

"With my iPhone, if I had their number, I could call anyone in the world.

"Here, our world is what we see in front of or behind us. In 2015, you can go anywhere in the United States in five or six hours unless you're talking about Alaska or Hawaii. In fact, Mom, Dad and I went to Hawaii once. We flew out of Chicago in the morning and were in Honolulu that afternoon."

"You could fly?" Mandy asked.

"I couldn't of course. They have a big thing called an airplane. Think of it like a big metal tube with wings. Inside the tube are seats and windows. Enough to hold four or five hundred people inside. And travel over five hundred miles in an hour."

"Did you have a boyfriend?"

"No, I dated a few boys, but none of them were special. I was too busy with sports to date much. I had chores on the farm before and after school. What happened with Jed was he asked if I knew how to milk since I lived on a dairy farm. I told him I could, but ours was done with milking machines. It was a slip up on my part, and I was going to tell him what I've just told you. I backed down when he said he wasn't sure he could keep the secret."

"Why did you decide to tell me?"

"Because I felt I could trust you, and I need someone to talk to."

"I'll keep your secret. How do you cope with something like this?"

"What else can I do? I go one day at a time and try not to be a bother to anyone."

"Would you go back if you could?"

"In a heartbeat. I want to know what happened to my parents. They wouldn't have been on that trip or that road if they hadn't been doing something for me. None of this would have happened. I feel responsible for it all."

"You shouldn't blame yourself," Mandy said.

"Maybe not, but I do."

Jed…

Jed rode up, dismounted and got a dipper of water. "Watch the cattle," he said. "See how much more lively they are? They can sniff the water. We're getting close; we'll be lucky if they don't run."

"If I get a whiff, I may run too," Angie said.

"I heard that," Mandy chimed in.

CHAPTER FOURTEEN

Green River

The meeting…

"Let me warn you folks," Major Adams said. "Green River is dangerous. It's wide, and where we'll cross is about twenty feet deep, so the wagons will have to be ferried across. It's going to take the better part of two days to do it, so take the time while you're waiting to get everything repaired, greased and tightened up. Be careful. Be out of the wagons while crossing, and hold onto something. We don't need a repeat of last time.

"So far we've been lucky and only had three accidents. We've lost four people since leaving Ohio. Other trains have lost many more. We've been fortunate in missing out on cholera for the most part. Get caught up on your rest and maintenance. We'll have one more day after everyone gets across. From here on, it's rough going with two major mountain ranges and a lot of water to cross. We've got about two more months on the trail. Good luck and Godspeed."

"You are looking better lately," Sophie Lewis told Polly Gilley.

"I'm feeling better. It's been over a week since I've been sick in the morning."

"That's good to hear. I had a touch of it with Mandy, but it only lasted a few days. With Jed there was never a bad day. After what you went through, I realize how lucky I was."

"It's been pretty bad. It would have been a lot worse without Angie. She's been a blessing. She does all of the laundry and cleaning up. She's been fixing most of the morning meals. She's doesn't know much about it, but bless her heart, she tries.

"I hope she finds a good man to marry. I know she's worried about what she's going to do when we get to Oregon."

"I've told her not to worry," Sophie said. "After what she did for Mandy, she's part of our family. I'm afraid she's too proud to accept help though. Lord knows, Jed would help her in a minute. I think he's in love with her."

"She's never said anything to me about him or anyone else," Polly replied.

"She told Jed she's not looking for a boyfriend."

"He's a nice boy. Maybe she'll change. I'll put a bug in her ear," Polly promised.

"Have you seen her shoes lately?" Sophie asked. "They were worn so thin you could read through them. Jed told me about them, and I repaired them once. He and Mandy had some kind of argument or something with her and they haven't talked much since. They never told me what it was all about."

"They've been walking together the past few days," Polly said. "Mandy and Angie have, I mean. Jed came over to see how she was."

That evening…

"What's all of the commotion about?" Angie asked, as the sounds of fiddles wafted over the camp, followed by the sounds of clapping hands.

"I'll bet they're having a dance," Polly replied. "Two or three people brought fiddles, and there are guitars and banjos. We had dances early on when we had a nice camping spot and were laying over. That was before people were so tired."

"Seth, let's go. I haven't felt like dancing in a long time. I'm probably as graceful as a cow now, but it might be fun to try."

"You've got a deal," he said.

"Angie, you come too," Polly said. "You haven't had a break in forever."

"You go ahead and enjoy yourselves. I'll just stay and straighten things around here."

"Nonsense," Polly told her. "You're coming. Seth, will carry you if it's the only way you'll come."

Seth grinned and stood, "Which is it going to be?" he asked.

"I'll go, I'll go. I don't want to be slung over your shoulder like a sack of potatoes," Angie said, laughing. "You shouldn't gang up on me. Two on one is not fair."

"Fairs got nothing to do with it. You deserve to have some fun."

A bonfire had been built in the middle of the circle using the now abundant wood. The livestock had been moved to the edge of the circle. The long dresses of the ladies stirred a cloud of dust that mingled with the smoke from the fire. A slight breeze was taking it away from the merrymakers.

Seth and Polly joined the couples in the middle when the fiddles and banjos began playing square dance music. "Would you like to dance?" Jed asked Angie, walking among the flickering shadows from the bonfire, startling her with his sudden appearance.

"I've never danced to this type of music," she said.

"Come on," he replied. "You'll be good, and if you aren't, it's too dark for anyone to notice. I'm a clodhopper myself."

She hesitated. "I don't know…"

"If you don't, I'll have to dance with Mama and Mandy. That would be embarrassing."

"I wouldn't want you to have to suffer the humiliation, but you can't laugh."

"I would never laugh at you, Angie."

After two dances, Jed said, "I don't want to get you over tired, since you've been sick. Come say hello to Mama and Papa."

"How did he convince you to dance?" Sophie asked.

Angie looked at Jed, and flashed a devilish grin. "He said if I didn't, he'd have to dance with you and Mandy. He sounded so pitiful, I couldn't refuse."

"He has to dance with me anyway," Mandy said. "Come on, little brother."

"I always wanted a brother or sister," Angie told Sophie, after Mandy led Jed to where the group was dancing to a reel.

"We wanted more, but it wasn't meant to be. At least we have those two," Sophie said. "I was going to ask how you're doing, but I can see you're better."

"I am better, thanks to all of the attention from these nice people.

"Did you see Polly and Seth dancing?" Angie asked.

"I did. It was good to see her feeling better. We had a nice visit earlier today."

"They're good people. I hope everything works out for them."

Jed and Mandy returned. "That was embarrassing," Jed said. "Everyone was laughing at me."

"That was because they've never seen anyone with two left feet try to dance before," Mandy replied.

"Angie, please come help me try to restore my reputation," Jed said.

Extending her hand, she asked, "Now I ask you, how can a girl resist that offer?"

"Do you think she's loosening up?" Sophie asked.

"I hope so," Mandy replied. "They'd be good together."

CHAPTER FIFTEEN

A Gift

The Green River Camp…

"Seth, I see some Indians coming this way. Should we do something?" Angie asked.

"No, we're fine. They've probably just come to trade. Several people traded with some of them back at Fort Laramie."

"Good. I was worried," she said.

"They have blankets, moccasins, things like that. Sometimes you can trade your tired horse for a fresh one."

Later…

"I enjoyed yesterday," she told Jed.

"It was fun. I'm glad you came out."

"I am too, although Polly and Seth threatened me if I didn't."

"Then I'll have to thank them for it. So we're friends again?" he asked.

"I never changed from being your friend. I was having a hard time and wanted to be alone, that's all."

"I've got big ears, so anytime you want someone to listen, I'm available."

"I'll keep it in mind. I'm hoping I don't get that way again."

"The Indians that were here earlier?"

"Yes, what were they doing?"

"They were just looking to do some trading. We traded some flour with them."

"What did you get?"

"These," he said and handed her a pair of moccasins.

"They're beautiful," she said. "You're going to look darling in them."

"I got them for you. Your shoes are worn out."

She made no move to take them. "You shouldn't have done that. I can't accept them."

"Why not?" he challenged. "You need them. I like you and I'm your friend. I want to help. Angie, for once don't let your stubborn pride get in the way. You saved my sister's life. I'm not trying to pay you for it, but I appreciate what you did, and I want to return the favor in a much smaller way."

She stood on tiptoe and kissed him on the cheek. "Thank you," she said, her voice choked with emotion.

"I'm never going to wash my face again," he told her, his cheeks flush with pleasure.

"You can wash it off, I'll replace it," she said.

"It's a deal."

"I want to try them on," she said.

"I'm pretty sure they'll fit. I used the memory of the foot rub. Besides, there wasn't a lot of choice in sizes, and these were the prettiest ones she had."

"I wonder what they're made of?" she asked.

"I can't tell. It's definitely not buffalo. I would guess deer, elk or maybe moose."

"They fit! Want to take a walk so I can try them out?"

Their walk took them to the center of the circle. A scruffy looking man wearing buckskins looked up as they approached. "I thought maybe you'd be wearing them Injun shoes you got," he said, and spat a stream of tobacco juice at the fire.

"Sorry to disappoint you. Angie, this is Slade, the scout I've been riding with. Slade, Angie Thornton. She's the one I got the moccasins for."

"I'm pleased to meet you, Mr. Slade." She pulled her skirt up enough to show her shoes. Aren't they pretty?"

"Yessum, they sure are. Made of moose hide, they are. I seen them make'em many a time. I speck they look a lot better on you than they would on ole Jed here."

"I would hope so," she laughed. "It's been nice meeting you, Mr. Slade. You be sure and take care of Jed for me when he's out with you."

"I shore will, ma'am. You kin count on that."

They continued the stroll around camp. "I'll bet he's seen a lot," Angie said.

"He has. He lived with the Shoshone's for a couple of years. He had a Shoshone wife, but she died of smallpox."

"I was vaccinated for smallpox, were you?"

"Before we left Ohio. Papa insisted we all get it."

"I agree with him on that." They continued walking. She slipped her hand in his. When he looked at her, she flashed a brilliant smile at him.

* * *

"Mama, look, you're not going to believe your eyes." Mandy pointed to the couple walking in their direction.

"Are they holding hands?" Sophie asked.

"Unless my eyes are deceiving, me that is exactly what they are doing."

"Polly and I talked about this the other day," Sophie said.

"Hi," Angie said gaily. "Do you know what your son did?"

"What did he do this time?" Sophie asked.

"He traded for these." Angie showed them the moccasins.

"Oh, I knew about those. Do they fit?"

"They do, and they're comfortable too."

"I saw them," Mandy said, "but I thought he was getting them for himself. He's always liked bright shiny things. I looked at what they had to trade, but nothing looked like it would fit me."

"I think walking is going to be more comfortable for me.

"I'm going to show them to Polly and Seth. Come on, go with me." Still holding hands, they walked through the shadows to the Gilley wagon.

"She's leading him around like he's got a ring in his nose," Mandy said.

"Mandy Lewis! Be ashamed of yourself," Sophie said.

"Oh Mama, I'm glad for him. He's been mooning around like a sick calf ever since she came. I've told her she wouldn't do any better than him. I just hope he doesn't get hurt."

"We learn from our mistakes, honey."

At the Gilley wagon…

"Polly, Jed got these shoes from the Indians today. Aren't they pretty?"

"They are. That was awfully sweet of you, Jed," Polly told him.

"Yes ma'am. I thought they'd look nice. I'd best be getting back."

Angie walked into the shadows with him. "Jed, thanks again and thanks for thinking of me." She kissed him on the cheek.

"You're about all I think of any more," he said.

"I think about you too. You're a nice person, and I'm glad you're my friend. Good night. And you can wash your cheek." She smiled and went back to the wagon.

"Do I detect a change in your feelings?" Polly asked.

"Maybe… a little. Good night, Polly."

CHAPTER SIXTEEN

Over the Mountains

"Good morning," Jed said. "Ready for another fifteen miles or so?"

"I guess. I don't have anything else planned for today," Angie said.

"You don't sound very happy this morning. Did I say something last night?"

"No, I'm just feeling sorry for myself again. The closer we get to the end, the more it bothers me."

""You're going to be all right. I'll see to that," he promised.

"How can you promise something like that?"

"Because I care for you."

"The right girl, someone you can really care for, is going to come along and knock your socks off, you wait and see."

"She already did," he replied, and went back to his place with the livestock as the wagons began to move out.

His remark stunned her. Other than her parents, no one had ever said anything like that to her. Several boys back in Brevard had asked her out, and she had gone a few times, but never more than once or twice with the same one. After she firmly rejected their clumsy attempts to make out, they never asked again. It hadn't mattered because she was determined to win a scholarship to save her parents the expenses of college.

"How do your new shoes feel?" She had not heard Mandy's approach.

"They make it more comfortable to walk. I don't feel every rock I step on any more. Did you have anything to do with it?"

"Nope, it was all his idea," Mandy replied. "He really cares for you."

"I know. He implied as much this morning. I told him the closer we get to where we're going, the more it bothers me. He told me he would make sure I would be all right No one's ever said anything like that to me before."

Two weeks later...

"We've got a little more than six weeks left on the trail," Polly said. "Seth and I have talked it over, and we'd like for you to be part of our family and live with us for as long as you like or need to.

"I'm not looking for a housekeeper or a nanny. You've won a place in our hearts. Seth and I both care for you very much."

"That is so kind of you. I've really been getting depressed by the thought of the end."

"It's not the end, Angie. It's a new beginning," Polly told her.

"I should look at it that way too, although my new beginning started when Jeremy found me."

That evening…

"Polly and Seth have invited me to live with them. So there's a little light at the end of the tunnel," Angie told Jed. "I just hope it's not on the front end of a train."

"Do you ever look at anything without doubts? Mama was going to invite you to live with us," he told her. "See, you have more than one choice."

"I'm overwhelmed by all this kindness to someone who is a stranger."

"You might have been a stranger at one time, but you're not anymore."

Touched by the sentiment, she took a step closer, laid her head on his shoulder. His arms found their way around her waist and shoulder hugged her.

"Thank you," she whispered. "I feel so secure right now."

"You are safe. Nothing is going to hurt you while I'm around."

She leaned back and looked into the dark pools of his eyes, seeing nothing but warmth and affection. Putting her hand behind his head, she pulled his lips to hers. The dry and cracked skin was warm to the touch.

"Mm," a throaty hum escaped her mouth, as she pressed herself against him. They broke the kiss. When she looked into his face again, she saw a look of dismay.

"I'm sorry," he apologized. "I shouldn't have let that happen. I shouldn't have taken advantage like that."

"If you remember, I started it. I wanted you to kiss me. Didn't you want to?"

"Well, yes, but a gentleman doesn't take advantage of a lady."

"When the lady wants it to happen, there's nothing wrong with it. It felt good. And right."

Fort Hall…

The Adams Caravan camped outside Fort Hall the last week in June. At a council of drivers, Major Adams addressed the group. "Our animals need some time to graze and let their sore feet heal. We're seven or eight weeks from Oregon City. I don't think we have to worry any more about being caught by the snows in the mountains. We may have a snowfall, but it won't be serious, just cold.

"Your biggest concern now is going to be building a shelter before winter. Replenish your supplies while we're here, and take care of your gear. Get rested and get ready for the next mountains."

After the meeting…

"Angie, I'm going to the Fort, come go with me," Jed said. "It will do you good to get away from the wagons for a while."

"Why? I can't buy anything?"

"It would give me the pleasure of your company," he told her. "I'm just going to look around and see what it's like. I'd like to see the inside.

"There's a Hudson Bay Trading Post. We're going back tomorrow for supplies."

"Let me see if Polly and Seth need for me to do anything. If they don't, then I will keep you company."

Polly said "There was nothing we need. You've done a lot. You and Jed go enjoy yourselves. Seth and I are going to see if the post doctor can see me, even though I'm doing a lot better."

"Are you sure you don't want me to stay and keep an eye on things while you're gone?"

"No," Polly answered. We'll button things up and tell our neighbors we're going to be gone."

In Fort Hall…

"It isn't as busy in here as the others," Angie observed.

"The Parting of the Ways took quite a few wagons to California before we got this far, so Fort Laramie was busier and bigger," he told her.

"Let's have something to eat while we're here. Mama's a good cook, but there's only so much you can do over an open fire."

"Why don't you go ahead, and I'll just take in the sights?"

"It wouldn't taste as good if you're not there to share it with me. When are you going to realize that people really care for you, and want to share with you?"

Her eyes misted. "I can't help it. I've always worked for everything I've had and now it's... It isn't the same."

He stopped in front of the small café. Come on. If you don't want to eat, you can watch me.

Seated at a small, somewhat rickety table, he looked at the menu scrawled on a small chalkboard. "What'll you folks have?" the blowsy waitress asked.

"Do you have lemonade?"

"No, but we do have tea."

"Bring two teas, please," he told her.

She turned and started to walk away. "Aren't you going to ask her what she wants?"

"Now ain't you the funny one?" the waitress said.

"I'm not being funny, I want two iced teas. Angie, what would you like?"

"I'll have tea also, please."

"Do you have eggs?" The waitress nodded. "I would like a steak with eggs. Angie?"

"I don't suppose you have any vegetables?"

"Hon, I suggest you go with what he did, the gardens ain't had time to bear yet, and what gets hauled in mostly goes to the Army."

"I'll go with that then. I haven't had an egg in months," she said.

"Angie, when we get to Oregon, most of us are probably going to settle in the same area. I'd like to call on you if it's all right with you."

"Don't take this the wrong way," she answered, "but what do you have in mind?"

"Well, when I just turned eighteen, so I'm going to be able to file on land. When you homestead, you have to live on it for five years. I like you. A lot. I expect to get married someday and have a family. I want you to be a part of it."

"That's a lot to digest. I won't be eighteen until January."

"Mama was only seventeen when she got married," he told her."

"I'm not your mother," she reminded him. "People mature at different ages. I'm not old enough to even think of getting married."

"You need to start thinking about it, what with all of your circumstances and everything."

Her eyes filled with tears. "I don't need to be reminded of my situation. I know well enough what it is. Nevertheless, I will not put myself into something as serious as marriage until I feel ready for it. I'm also thinking of you when I say this."

"I didn't mean to upset you. I don't want to rush you into anything. I'm just saying…"

"Jed, don't make it worse by trying to explain. If you want me to be your friend, then fine. If you want me for a wife, it's way too early for me to even think about something like that. I may not even be cut out to be a wife. It's something I have to figure out for myself. I only plan to marry once in my life and I want it to be right."

"I guess I missed something somewhere," he said. I thought you liked me."

"I do like you, but don't misread like for love."

"Aren't they the same?"

CHAPTER SEVENTEEN

Love Is…

Love and like…

"In my mind, love and like are not the same. Love means making yourself vulnerable. You put your heart and soul on the line. When you love someone, you're setting yourself up to be hurt, but you don't care. It's worth the risk, no matter what.

"Like means you enjoy someone's company, and want to do things with them. My mother told me liking someone comes before loving them.

"Mom and Dad didn't even have to talk to express their love. When she passed his chair, she would touch his arm or shoulder. He gave his life for her. That's what love is to me."

"I don't know anything about any of that," he said. "I just know I like you and want to be with you.

"You didn't eat very much of your dinner."

"I never eat every much unless there are vegetables. Why don't you eat it or take it with you? Maybe your mother or father would like it."

"They will probably eat here too," he said. "What does vulnerable mean?"

"It means putting yourself in a position where you can be hurt. Either physically or emotionally. For example, when you said you liked me, it made you vulnerable. Or, if you have to get in front of a herd of buffalo, you're vulnerable."

"I'd also be crazy," he said.

"That too," she said, laughing.

"Give the food to Seth and Polly," he said. I can't be eating too much of this store bought food."

"I'm going to have to work vulnerable into a conversation with Mandy."

"Just tell her you're vulnerable, and play it from there."

"You do have a sense of humor, don't you?" he asked.

"I try, but sometimes it's hard. I hope I didn't hurt your feelings, but I just... I don't know. I tried to be honest with you."

"I'm disappointed, but you didn't hurt my feelings. I'm not giving up though."

"Good."

"Let's walk through the Hudson Bay place," he suggested.

"Sounds like a plan."

* * *

The wagon wheels were rolling again, headed for the Snake River. Twenty five miles later, they made camp at the American Falls. "Good grass and good water," Slade reported.

The following day ate up another twenty-two miles that involved crossing several streams that emptied into the Snake. They camped with a train of freight haulers eastbound.

"If you have any letters, they've agreed to put them in the mail when they pass the Pony Express Station," Jed said. "Angie, if you want to write someone, just give it to me and I'll take it to them. They're a pretty rough bunch, so I'll save you any contact." He leaned over and whispered, "I know you don't have the means, so I'll take care of the postage."

He wasn't prepared for the wave of sadness that washed over her face. "What's the matter? Did I say something wrong?"

She shook her head and said, "No," then turned away.

"I don't know what I did," he told Mandy. "I offered to mail anything she wanted to send back home. Honestly, I don't understand her. I'm always upsetting her one way or another. Maybe it would be best if I just didn't say anything."

"You didn't do or say anything, Jed. She doesn't have anyone left to write."

"I didn't know that. I sure stepped in it this time," he said.

"It's not your fault any more than it is hers. You just go on being nice. She's having a really hard time."

Later…

The camp had settled in for the night when a series of shots rang out from the area where the stock was bedded down. From her sleeping place under the wagon, Angie watched the men running to the sound.

"What's going on?" she asked Seth, as he got out of the wagon and pulled his shoes on.

"Sounds like someone's after the horses," he answered and ran to the commotion.

Within minutes, he was back, leading one of his horses. He saddled the horse and rode off with nine other men. "Indians are trying to run off with the horses," he shouted.

It was three hours before the men returned. During their absence, the freighters had harnessed their oxen and headed east for Fort Hall, leaving only the wagons of Major Adams caravan.

The Indian rustlers had driven the horses and cattle into a box canyon, and set up an ambush for their pursuers at the entrance. Two members of the caravan had been shot in the melee, one of whom was Seth

Gilley. Two horses had been lost, driven off by escaping Indians.

The wounded were brought back to camp. Mrs. Parsons was called to look at Seth.

"Son," she said to Jed, "get me some whiskey. Miz Gilley, can you git me a piece of cloth or something for him to bite on."

They sprang to do her bidding. "Is there anything I can do?" Angie asked.

"When I get him drunk enough, I'm gonna need a hot iron to cauterize the hole the arrow made." Angie went for the iron.

Four men were enlisted to hold Seth down. "Git me the hot iron," Mrs. Parsons directed.

""I'll help you," Jed told Angie. He put a rod that was used to stir the fire into the hot coals.

"What is she going to do?" she asked Jed.

"She's going to use the iron to cauterize where the arrow hit."

"She's going to burn him?"

"They do it to stop the bleeding and try to keep it from getting infected."

"I don't want to watch this," she said.

"You stay with Miss Polly and Mama. I'm going to help hold him down."

Seth's scream when the hot iron was applied to the wound drowned all other sounds, until mercifully, he passed out. Polly and Angie were both crying, holding each other.

"How are we going to manage without him to do for us?" Polly asked.

"Don't worry, we'll manage," Angie said. "You just worry about yourself and Seth. I'll take care of everything else," Angie told her.

The next morning…

Major Adams called for a layover the next day to allow the wounded a chance to recover. Angie and Polly had packed the things they had used to prepare the food. "Angie, I don't have any idea what to do in order to move out."

Jed walked up to them. "Miss Polly, you stay in the wagon and take care of Seth. I'll get the oxen hitched, and we'll be ready to go." He tied the horse to the back of the wagon, and hitched the oxen. The other wagons began moving, with the Gilley wagon falling about one hundred yards behind.

"Thank you Jed. We would have been left behind," Angie said, walking alongside as he led the oxen.

"You wouldn't have been left. Major Adams wouldn't have let that happen. I wouldn't have either, for that matter. I had told him I would be here."

"I'm grateful," she said.

"I don't want to get surprised by anyone trying to take advantage of us as stragglers so keep an eye out to the side and back until we catch up.

"Do you think they might come back?"

"I doubt it, but if we see anything, I'll get the attention of the others by firing the rifle."

Groans came from the wagon as Seth regained consciousness. "That just chills my soul," Angie said. "He must be in terrible pain."

She heard Polly trying to comfort her husband.

CHAPTER EIGHTEEN

The Barlow or the River

The trail more or less followed the Snake River for more than three hundred miles over a three-week span.

"I think the closer we get to Oregon, the worse the roads are," Angie observed. She was startled as Seth screamed after the wagon rolled over a rock.

"I feel sorry for him," Jed observed. "I know he feels bad about having to rely on someone to do things he feels he should be doing. It wouldn't do any good to tell him though. It's got to be rough on Miss Polly too. Being great with child, she has to be uncomfortable, but I haven't heard one word of complaint from her. All of the jarring and bumping must be getting her down, but she doesn't let him see it."

"That's one of her ways of showing her love for him. She's more concerned for him than she is for herself." Angie looked at Jed. "That's love. She loves him with everything she has, with no regard for herself."

"Don't take this wrong, but shouldn't she be concerned for her baby too?"

"She is," Angie said. "We talked about it the other night. She doesn't want to let him know because she doesn't want to add to his pain."

"Is there anything else we can do to help?" he asked.

"If there is, I don't know what it is." She looked at his face. *He is sincere and he cares. There's more to him than I thought. I shouldn't be surprised. Mandy is the same way and so is their mother. They have surely been nice to me.*

* * *

A council meeting…

"We're finally done with the Snake," Major Adams told them. "We've got about five days along the Burnt River to the Powder, and then eight or ten days to the Dalles. There's a trading post there and according to my guide book, you can take a boat down the Columbia or take the Barlow Road. The book says the Barlow is one of the hardest parts of the trail."

"Wouldn't that take a lot of boats to carry the wagons?" Harve Winston asked.

"Here's the thing, Harve," Major Adams said. "It's expensive on the river. The book says fifty dollars a wagon, and ten dollars a person. That's probably changed, more than likely gone higher. The other way is the Barlow Road around the south flank of Mount Hood. It says the roads are poor, and steep. They're hard on the livestock.

"The way I feel is, I wouldn't want to get to the end with nothing left and winter coming. I would take the road and save the money. It won't be easy and we've got the Blue Mountains and the Cascades ahead of us. One other thing, there is a five dollar toll on the Barlow."

The Lewis family…

"I'm thinking hard about the river route," Hiram Lewis told his family that night. "Clint said the book says it's much easier and saves time."

"We could save a good bit of money going by land," Jed said. "We've already come through some rough times. We can handle the mountains."

"We have had it rough at times. Maybe it's time for us to take it easy," Hiram said.

"I'm going to stay with Angie and the Gilley's. I don't think they can afford to pay that much, even if it would be easier."

"Think about what you're saying, son. We could be there and working on shelter before the train even gets there," Hiram told him.

"I'm going overland," Jed said, with finality.

"I'm proud of you," Mandy said.

"If you try to kiss me, I'll slug you," he promised.

The next morning…

"Did Polly and Seth talk about going on the river or over the mountains?" Mandy asked Angie.

"They did, but said they didn't want to use any more money than they had to. I wonder what they would do if I weren't here."

"You've earned your way several times over," Mandy assured her. "Papa's thinking about it, but Jed flat out said he's going over land. He said he didn't think they could afford it, even if it would be easier on them both."

"That's so sweet," Angie said.

"That's so like Jed," Mandy told her. "I told him I was proud of him."

"What did he say?"

Mandy grinned. "He said if I tried to kiss him, he'd slug me."

"Wonder if he'd slug me?"

"Try it and see," Mandy said.

"I just might."

That evening…

After Jed had taken on the task of leading the Gilley oxen when Seth had been injured, they spent more time together. They began taking walks in the evening after Seth resumed leading his team.

"Mandy told me what you said last night," Angie said.

"Mandy's got a big mouth. It's going to get her in trouble someday."

She stopped and looked up at him. "Jed?" She wrapped her arms around his neck, pulled his head down and kissed him on the lips.

He was flabbergasted, and at a loss for words. "You didn't slug me," she said.

"What?"

"Mandy said you told her you'd slug her if she tried to kiss you. You didn't slug me."

His cheeks were flame red. He looked around.

"What's the matter?" she asked.

"What if someone saw that?" he asked. "What would they think?"

"They would think it was a boy kissing his girl. Does that bother you? What they think, I mean?"

"I wouldn't want them to think I was trying to force myself on you."

"If they were watching, they would have seen it was the other way around. I'm not ashamed of it. What if I yelled it out? Would that embarrass you?"

"You wouldn't do that."

"Dare me?"

"I don't know what you mean," he said.

"When you dare someone to do something, they're a coward if they don't do it."

"Well, I'm not going to dare you."

An impish grin spread across her face, causing her green eyes to sparkle. "I would."

"You wouldn't," he said.

"Dare me," she challenged.

CHAPTER NINETEEN

This is Me

Jed didn't pick up the gauntlet she had thrown down. "I don't think I will do that."

"I started to tell you something a while back, but when you didn't promise to keep it a secret, I held back. Instead, I told Mandy. She and Major Adams are the only people I've told what I'm going to tell you now. I trust you enough to keep it to yourself.

"You will have trouble believing what I'm about to say, but it is the truth. If you can believe it, then it will explain many of the strange things that surround me. Don't interrupt me and I'll try to answer any questions you have when I'm finished.

First, my name is Angela Thornton and my parents and I were caught in a flash flood. We had gone from Brevard to the University of Nebraska in Lincoln. I was a good athlete in high school. Just in case you don't know, an athlete is someone who is good in sports.

"I was better than good. I was very good, good enough that several colleges wanted to pay for my college tuition and expenses just to play for their schools. I can probably outrun you, and out jump you. We both know I can swim better than you.

"Anyway, we were on our way home when Dad hit water flowing across the road and lost control of the car and we went into the flood waters. We weren't in a wagon. We were in a car." He started to say something, but she held up her hand to stop him.

"A car is a machine that is driven by an engine running on gasoline. They can travel fast. Really fast. It took us about three hours to go the 200 miles to Lincoln.

"When we hit the water, the car began floating in the current. I managed to climb through a window and onto the top of the car. Dad was trying to help Mom get out. They were both knocked into the water by an overhanging limb. I don't think they made it. The same limb hit me, but I managed to hold on. I was caught in a notch of the tree. That's where Jeremy found me."

"Angie, it hadn't rained for days when we found you."

"Think back… I asked Major Adams to feel my shoes. They were wet."

"Yes, but…"

"Let me go on. I'm seventeen years old. I was born January 27… 1998. In Brevard, Missouri."

"That's impossible."

She looked to see if anyone was around. They were alone, so she pulled her iPhone from her pocket. It was fully charged.

"This is called an iPhone. It's made by a company called Apple and won't be invented for another one hundred-forty years. With it, I could have talked to anyone in the world if I had their telephone number. It says "No service" now because there are no others yet to connect with."

She touched the illuminated screen in several places. "This is our house, and the red thing is one of our cars. The one we were riding in when we went into the water. This is a picture of my Mom and Dad." She swiped her finger across the screen and Major Adams' picture appeared. One more swipe and there was the picture of a puzzled Mandy beside Angie.

"Come close to me, and put your arm around my waist. Closer than that. Come on. Act like you mean it."

She held the iPhone in front of her. The bright flash startled Jed, and caused Angie to smile. "Look at this."

The image of the two of them stared Jed in the face. "That is absolutely unbelievable," he said, emphasizing each word."

"There is a lot more I could tell you that would be more unbelievable. Now you know just about everything there is to know about Angela Thornton. It's up to you whether to believe it or not. I know you have doubts, so it's all right with me if you want to talk to Mandy. She promised not to talk about it with anyone, but I'll tell her it's okay to talk to you."

"I don't understand any of this," he said.

"You don't understand it? Try living it. I don't know whether my parents are living or dead or in still another time."

"What was it like?"

"There's so much difference, it's hard to pick any one thing. Incredible things have happened." She pointed to the moon overhead. "Men from the United States will go there in 1969, walk on the surface and come back to earth."

"As strange as it all sounds, I believe you," Jed said. "It does explain a lot of things."

"Thank you. It's important to me that you do believe me."

The next morning…

"Papa has decided to go the Barlow Road," Mandy told Angie.

"Why did he change his mind?"

"He found out the river is easier going, but dangerous. There are several falls. The main thing was everyone else is going on the Barlow, and he didn't want to give up his friends."

"I'm glad you're going this way. You and Jed are the only friends I have. I like Polly and Seth, but it's different.

"By the way, I told Jed my story last night, so it's okay for you to talk to him about it. He had trouble believing it at first, but I think he did."

"You are getting along pretty well with him aren't you?"

"Yes. I like him. In fact, I like him a lot. It isn't love yet, but it could be some day. Compared to him, I feel like a girl."

"Actually, he was born in '48. You're 148 years older."

"I know. Right now, my feet feel every year too. Physically he's seven or eight months older, but it seems a lot more.

"That's strange, isn't it? I guess it's because of where I came from. Boys become men quicker now than in my time."

"This is your time now," Mandy reminded her.

"I know that, but I still think I might wake up and find is all a dream. A long dream that is tougher than anything I could have imagined."

"Don't let him get away. You won't find a nicer boy anywhere," Mandy told her.

"That's part of my problem. He's not a boy, he's a man, and I'm not ready for a relationship with a man."

CHAPTER TWENTY

The Home Stretch

The end of the Barlow Road…

"Less than a week left on the trail," Angie said to Jed. "What is it going to be like to wake up knowing we don't have to walk fifteen or twenty miles?"

"Heaven. It's going to be heaven. We're out of the mountains and the hills are becoming less steep," he told her. "Tomorrow, the last of them will be behind us. Slade says two days to Sandy and one more to Oregon City.

"What's going to happen between us when we get there?" he asked.

"I was hoping you wouldn't bring that up. I'm still too young to think about getting married and I don't think I will be for a while."

"Do I even have a chance?" he asked.

She looked at the earnest face. "Jed, you're the only person that has a chance. I care for you, and I like you a lot. Goodnight," she said, elevating to her toes for the night kiss that had become a nightly ritual.

They kissed. "Goodnight." He turned to head back to his family's wagon. He stopped. "Angie, I love you with all of my heart, and I will take care of you."

It was the first time she had ever heard the words from anyone other than her relatives. *I think I love you too.* It was a sentiment she was unable to say aloud.

"Goodnight, Polly," her voice choked with emotion.

Polly peered through the opening in the rear covering of the wagon. "Are you all right? You sound strange."

"I'm fine," Angie replied.

"You don't sound fine. What's wrong?"

"Jed just told me he loves me."

"Then you should be happy instead of being sad. It's a magical time. I remember the first time Seth told he loved me."

"That's just it. I can't let myself fall in love with him."

"It sounds as if it's too late for you to think that way. You'll be fine. You have a home with us, and they'll be just down the road when you realize how you feel, and are ready to admit it."

"I wish it was that simple. Goodnight, Polly."

Three days later, they were in Oregon City.

The Lewis family and the Gilley's got together over supper. Hiram led the discussion. "We've taken a house and barn on the edge of town from a man that's gone off to the gold fields, and we plan to move tomorrow. We will be staying there until we have a place of our own. Seth and Polly have a room here in the boarding house.

"We've made some tentative plans. We're going to give our weary feet a rest for a couple of days. After that, we want to go look at likely areas to settle. Since we want to be close to Seth and Polly, We have no idea how long we'll be gone, so I've hired one of the settler's sons to look after the stock while we're gone. When we come back, we should have an idea where we are going to be living. In the meantime, Angela, it is not my place to give you orders, but if you're willing to listen to a suggestion, I have one.

"While we're gone, Polly will stay in the house with Sophie. You can share Mandy's room in the house. This way, Polly will have someone around in case she needs help, and it will also help them save some money. When we get back, we'll figure out what to do next. What do you think?"

"Mr. Hiram, I don't really have any choice. You're all being kinder to me than anyone has a right to expect, and I appreciate you sharing with me until I have the means to repay you."

"Dear," Sophie said gently, "the good Lord has provided well for us, and it is only right and proper we share it with you. We will not hear anything about repayment."

"Mr. Lewis, I accept your kind offer," Angie said.

"I share Angela's sentiment," Seth said.

"I've always wanted a sister and now I have one," Mandy said.

Later…

"Everything's all worked out," Jed told Angie.

"It isn't all worked out," she said. "I'm still living off the charity of others. It isn't something I want."

"That's just not true," he said. "You're helping take care of Miss Polly."

"And your father is helping take care of all of us."

"Like Mama said, we've been blessed, and it's right and proper, and besides, I love you."

"I love you too, but I don't want charity."

He heard only the first four words. He picked her up and whirled her around, his face all smiles. "It won't be charity if we're married."

"Put me down you idiot. What are other people going to think?"

"I don't care, do you?"

"No, but I'm still too young to get married."

"That's all right. I can wait. As long as you need me to, I'll wait." He set her back on the ground, but held onto her. "You'll think this is silly, but every night I have prayed for this."

"It's not silly at all," she said. "Now I want to be kissed."

With his arms wrapped around her, he bent, when his lips touched hers the fireworks went off in his head, sending jolts of electricity coursing through his body.

When they broke the kiss, she said, "That was nice."

"It was more than nice, it was wonderful," he corrected.

Angie was almost asleep in her usual place under the wagon when she sensed someone nearby. "I seen you and that boy, and I come for my share," a slurred voice said.

She screamed and tried to scramble further under the wagon, but he caught her ankle. "You can't get away from ole Burl," the coarse voice said. He had a terrible stench and reeked of rotgut whiskey.

Angie screamed again as he began pulling her from under the wagon.

"That's Angie!" Jed shouted, and ran toward the Gilley wagon. He charged into the drunk, and knocked the foul smelling man off his feet. She was free.

"Get away, Angie," Jed's voice said.

"Boy, you fooling with a man now," Burl roared, and swung his arm. He backhanded Jed and sent him sprawling. He grabbed a shovel from the side of the wagon and hit Jed on the side of his head. Burl leered, an evil grin as he drew back to hit Jed again. "You gonna get your comeuppance now, boy." A blast from

Hiram's double barrel shotgun hit him in the chest, driving him backwards and onto his back. The shovel fell harmlessly to the ground. Burl didn't move again, as his life's blood poured onto the ground.

Seth had jumped from his wagon, his rifle in his hands. Major Adams came running up. "What's going on?"

Hiram said "We heard Angie screaming. Jed got here first and hit this man at a dead run. He hit Jed with a shovel and was fixing to hit him again when I let go with my shotgun. He's not from our company, so he wasn't up to any good.

"I got to see to Jed. I think he's hurt bad," Hiram said.

Polly was struggling to climb down from the wagon and would have fallen if Seth hadn't caught her.

Sophie was kneeling on the ground beside Jed. "Hiram, we need to get him to the doctor. They do have one here don't they?"

"I'm sure they do. I'll get hitched," Hiram said and ran toward his wagon.

Meanwhile, Major Adams said, "Miss Thornton, what happened here?"

"I was just about asleep when this... he grabbed me and was trying to pull me from under the wagon. Jed knocked him loose and told me to run. The next thing I know, the gun went off."

"Why were you under the wagon this time of the night?" Major Adams asked.

"It's where I sleep," she said.

"Major, she won't have it any other way," Seth said.

"No more," Miss Thornton, understand?"

"She's going to be staying with us in our rent house, Major," Sophie said.

Hiram and Seth loaded Jed in the wagon pulled by horses he had borrowed, since they would be faster than the oxen. Hiram boosted Sophie to the wagon, along with Mandy."

"May I go too, Mr. Hiram?" a trembling Angie asked.

"Sure, honey. I'll give you a boost." He shook the reins and they clattered off toward the center of Oregon City, where they hoped to find a doctor.

CHAPTER TWENTY-ONE

It's Bad

Doctor Seamus Murphy…

Hiram stopped the wagon in front of Doctor Seamus Murphy's office on Main Street. He enlisted the help of a man passing by to get Jed inside.

"Put him on the table," directed the man who identified himself as Doctor Murphy. "What happened to this young man?" the gray-haired man asked as he donned a white smock to protect his clothes."

"He was hit in the head with a shovel," Hiram said.

"Is he going to be all right?" his anxious mother asked.

"I won't know until I've examined him," the kindly doctor replied. "Why don't you wait outside until I take a look at him?"

"We're his parents and we want to stay with him," Sophie replied. "Mandy, you and Angie wait outside."

"Yes ma'am."

"This could be very bad or nothing more than a bad headache. We don't know much about the brain, and I've never done any type of surgery," Dr. Murphy explained. "He has a large knot, but I don't see any evidence of bleeding. When he's a little more alert, I'll do some more checks. I think it would be best to keep him here at least for tonight where I can keep an eye on him."

"Will it be all right if I stay?" Sophie asked.

"Yes, it would be all right."

Sophie told the girls what the doctor had told her. "I'm going to stay with him tonight," she told them.

"Mrs. Lewis, I can stay. It's my fault he's here," Angie said.

"Why in the world would it be your fault?" Sophie asked. "Put that thought from your mind right now. You can stay, but I will stay with you."

Dr. Murphy brought another chair into the room. "He's trying to wake up." I don't want him to get up. His balance might not be good, and I don't want him falling and hitting his head again."

"We won't let him do that," Sophie said.

"Doc, we were going out to look at some claims in the morning, I guess he shouldn't do that, right?"

"I would advise doing nothing that might get him another hit on the head."

"Sophie, I'm going to check on the stock. Why don't you come with me and let the kids stay with Jed?"

"No," she said fiercely. "I'm staying with my boy."

Later…

"He really cares for you," Sophie said.

"I know," Angie answered. "I care for him too. In fact, earlier tonight, I told him I loved him too, but I wasn't ready to get married."

"Why don't you think so? I was about your age when Hiram and I married."

"I guess it's the way I was raised. I don't feel like I'm old enough to take on the responsibilities of being a wife. He seems like he's a lot older than me. I told him and he said he'd wait until I was ready."

"That's right smart of you to think about whether you're ready. It's a big step. The most important one a woman can take. I saw a few that married before they grew into adults, and it was a mess. You'll know when it's right. If it isn't Jed, you'll know that too."

She went to the bedside. He was awake. "Mama, is Angie all right?"

"Ask her yourself. She's right here."

"Angie's here?"

"I'm right here. You're my hero!"

"He didn't hurt you?"

"Thanks to you, he didn't have a chance. You gave me the chance to get away."

"I told you I wouldn't let anything happen to you."

"That's right, you did say that." She kissed him on the cheek.

"You be careful, he might come back."

"He won't bother anyone again, ever," his mother said.

"Is he…"

Sophie nodded. "How are you feeling?"

"Other than a bad headache, I'm fine. My first night in Oregon City and I'm spending it in the doctor's office."

"At least you're not sleeping on the ground," Angie said.

"Speaking of that, I didn't know you had been sleeping on the ground," Sophie said.

"It wouldn't have been right for me to displace Seth, so I insisted."

"You could have been in the wagon with Mandy and me," Sophie said.

"That wouldn't have been right either."

"You are the strangest girl I've ever met," Sophie said.

"That's me, Strange Angela Thornton."

"The Major was surprised when he found out where she had been sleeping and told her she is not to sleep under the wagon again," Sophie told Jed.

"I can hardly wait to get out and look around," Jed told them.

"It's going to be a few days before you can do much. The doctor says you can't take a chance on falling or anything."

"I'm fine," he insisted.

"We're going to go by what he said."

"That means I won't be able to go with Papa and Mr. Gilley to look at claims."

"Until the doctor says it's okay, that is the way it is. The subject is closed."

The next morning…

"Seth and I went by the land office today and found out what we have to do to file a claim. While we were there we looked at their map," Hiram told them. "We saw some likely looking places we are going to look."

"You can't wait until I can go?" Jed pleaded.

"There's another train coming in every day," Hiram said. "That means another thirty or forty people looking for land."

"Yes sir, I understand."

* * *

"How are you feeling this morning?" Dr. Murphy asked when he came in to check on his patient.

"Except for a headache, I feel pretty good," Jed replied.

"Have you tried sitting up?"

"Yes sir."

"Did you feel dizzy?"

"No sir."

"I don't think there's any need to keep you here any longer. You just need to be careful."

"Doctor, we were planning to start looking for a place to settle. Will he be able to go?" Hiram asked.

"I'd say give it the rest of the day and he should be good to go tomorrow, as long as he doesn't do any hard riding until the lump on his head goes down."

"Yes sir. I'll be careful," Jed promised.

"Son, it wouldn't be a good idea to get hit in the head by a shovel anytime soon either," Dr. Murphy told him, smiling.

"No sir. I plan to stay away from shovels for a while."

The wagon had been emptied and cleaned. They would sleep in real beds tonight.

CHAPTER TWENTY-TWO

Our Place

Thirty-five miles from Oregon City, and two days in the saddle brought the land hunters to Salem, the capitol, where they visited the land office. The next day, based on information from the clerk, they headed northwest to an area they deemed ideal. The land was located twelve miles from Salem. Silver Rock Creek wound its way through the area, and the soil looked fertile and plow ready.

"Seth, this is it for us," Hiram said. "I'm going to file on two sections, and buy another section."

"I don't think we'll do any better," Seth agreed.

At the land office in Salem, the paperwork was completed. "What about you, young man?" the clerk asked Jed. "Are you eighteen?"

"Yes sir, but I'm not married, so I don't qualify."

"The law says you have to be eighteen and you have to begin living on the land within six months. It would be a household of one, and you would be the head. I'll take your claim."

"Go for it, son," Hiram said.

When they left, Hiram and Sophie had three sections along Silver Rock Creek, including the one Hiram purchased. Jed had one section, and the Gilley's had two. All three sections had water and trees, along with what would be good pasture land.

"I don't believe it," Jed proclaimed. "I have a farm!"

"Is there any labor for hire around here?" Hiram asked the clerk.

"Yes sir, I believe you can find some of the Chinese that will hire out. Why do you ask?"

"I'd like to get started on a house, as soon as possible. Are there any places to rent?"

"There may be. There is a boarding house."

"Let's take a room tonight and head back in the morning," Hiram suggested.

* * *

Oregon City…

"We have good news and bad news. We filed claims on two sections and bought another," Hiram told friends and family at the supper table.

"On top of that, Jed was able to file a claim on a section. Seth filed on two sections"

"That's the good news. What's the bad?" Sophie asked.

"It's about fifty miles away. That means three more days in a wagon," Hiram told them.

"Three days I can do, after all we have been through, three more won't even be noticeable," she said.

"How are you feeling, Jed?" Angie asked.

"I'm tired, but I'm good. I missed you," he answered.

"I missed you too. I'm glad you're back. I've been kind of worried about you."

"Take note of this, everyone," Sophie said. "We're all going on about land, and this sweet girl is the only one asking about our son's well being. I'm embarrassed."

Angie's cheeks colored. "I was afraid he might have gotten woozy or something."

"Whatever woozy is, if it means dumb, he has it," Mandy said.

"Woozy means dizzy."

"He's that too."

"Stop picking on Jed. He saved my life," Angie told them.

"Now she's defending him," the undeterred Mandy said.

"Why wouldn't I? I love him." Angie retorted.

"Could we change the subject?" Jed asked. "You're going to love it. It's prettier than anything around here.

Besides, Most of the good land around here has already been taken."

"When are we going to see it?" Sophie asked.

"Why don't we plan to pack the wagon and head on down this week?" Hiram asked.

"Honey, are we going to be close to them?" Polly asked Seth.

"We'll be next-door neighbors. Jed will be on one side and we're on the other."

"I'm glad to hear that," she said.

"While we were there, I asked about a doctor, and there is one in Salem, about twelve miles away. Salem is the state capitol and is about the size of Oregon City, but not as large as Portland."

"There's plenty of timber, and a couple of sawmills not too far way. I think we'll have time for a late garden and winter wheat," Hiram said.

"How long will it take us to get winter shelter?" Sophie asked.

"We should be in within two months. I'm going to hire some help to work on that, so we'll have time to get everything done."

* * *

"You said you loved me. Does this mean you changed your mind about marrying me?"

"Not unless you ask me. That is if you ever get around to it."

"Angie, will you be my wife?" he asked, his nerves revealed by the quaver in his voice."

"I will, but I want to wait until we have our own place. I love your family, but it would be crowded, and might be embarrassing at times."

He blushed, taking her meaning. He looked around, no one was watching so he took her into his arms and kissed her. His tongue traced the soft fullness of her lips. Her head reeled as spirals of pleasure raced through her veins. While his lips massaged hers, she pressed her body against him. She could feel the firm bulge pressing against her midsection. They broke the kiss, but the memory lingered in her mind.

"You had better hold me up," she said. "That buckled my knees."

"I can't believe the prettiest girl in the state just agreed to be my wife."

"You don't know that. You haven't seen all of the girls in the state."

"I've seen enough to know you're the prettiest. I'm going to take care of you and protect you. I'll be the best husband possible to you."

"I'll make you a good wife. With the examples I've had, how can I go wrong?"

"When do you want to tell the family?" he asked.

"What's wrong with now?"

"Good question," he said.

The assembled family...

"Now that we made our way here, and have filed our claim, I have something to tell you. A little while ago, I proposed to Angie and she accepted. We will be married when our cabin is ready to be lived in."

"Angie, did you get a bump on your head too, and taken leave of your senses." Mandy asked.

"Mandy, you apologize right now," Sophie said.

"Angie, I'm sorry you've taken leave of your senses," the undeterred Mandy said.

"Will you stay with us in the meantime?" Sophie asked.

"If you will have me."

"Then it's a done deal," Sophie said. "I'm happy for you, and if he gives you any problems, let me know. He's not too old for me to spank."

CHAPTER TWENTY-THREE

Planning

Haynes' Mill…

The two-wagon caravan made camp outside Salem midday on Tuesday. Hiram and Jed planned to sleep in the barn rented for their belongings. Sophie and the two girls were staying in rooms at the same boarding house where Seth and Polly were staying.

The next morning they set out to see their land. They ferried across the Willamette River and headed west from Salem.

"This is Haynes' Mill. A man named Abner Haynes has a lumber mill on the creek down-stream from us. We can cut timber and float the logs down the creek to the mill to have them cut into lumber for the house," Hiram told them. "Seth and Polly will be right below us while Jed and Angie are above."

"There's where our claim starts," Jed said, pointing ahead. He could not control his excitement as the trail curved around a bend in the creek. "What do you think?" he asked Angie.

"It's beautiful," she said. "It looks like it needs one pass with a plow and we'll be ready to plant."

"Yeah. I love it. There's plenty of trees to build a cabin. I probably won't have to go too deep to hit water either."

"How far are we from town?" she asked.

"I reckon we're about ten miles, don't you think, Papa?"

"That would be my guess," Hiram said.

"I have to start living here within six months," Jed said. "I'll have to start cutting logs for a cabin pretty soon."

Breakfast...

"Your mother talked about it last night, and for your wedding present, we're going to have the same crew that will lay out our cabin, do the same for yours. That will get the walls up and a roof on. We should both be able to move in less than two months.

"We'll need to get a barn up at our place for our stock, and then we can start with yours. We still have time to get winter wheat planted."

"Papa, you and Mama are the best," Angie said. "Oh, I should have asked first. Is it all right if I call you Papa and Mama?"

"We'd be honored," Sophie said. "Truth be told, I was going to suggest it. Being called Miss Sophie didn't sound right."

The weather cooperated, and both cabins had walls and a roof up in five weeks. Rocks for the chimneys were found and hauled to both home sites. "What's next?" Angie asked as they sat on the logs Jed had rolled in to use as chairs.

"We have to chink the walls and finish the fireplace and chimney." Jed told her.

"I don't know what chinking is," she confessed.

"The wind can get in through cracks between the logs, and it would be cold," he told her. "I'll stuff the cracks with mud and twigs to seal it as much as possible. After that, I'll be putting boards on the inside walls, but I can do that in any kind of weather."

"I can help do this chinking thing," Angie said.

"Honey, your hands are too nice to be dabbling in mud and sticking it in the walls. I don't want you to do that."

"When I was a little girl. I played in the mud all the time. You just called me honey. Do you realize it's the first time you've done that? Just so you know, if you think I'm going to sit around looking prim and pretty, you've got another think coming. This is going to be my house too, and I want to help. I will help.

"I just thought of something. Where are we going to sleep and what are we going to use for a table?"

"Me and Papa are going to build bed frames, and a table. I don't know what we'll do about a mattress. Theirs came out in the wagon, so they're okay, but they'll have to get one for Mandy.

"After we're married, we'll need to file for another section and double the size of our farm."

"At least I'll be bringing something to our marriage," she said.

"You're bringing yourself. That's good enough for me. The only regret I have is you were used to things being so much nicer than what we'll have."

"You listen to me. I walked from Missouri, a lot of the steps with shoe soles no thicker than a piece of paper, until you gave me the moccasins. Of course it was nicer then, but those times no longer exist for me. This is my time now. Our love for each other will make up for those things. I don't want you thinking that way anymore."

She stood, and then sat in his lap. "Kiss me," she commanded.

He wrapped his arms around her and teased her by barely touching her lips with his. "That ain't going to get it done, farm boy." She attacked his mouth with a hunger that surprised her. She moved his hand from her shoulder to her breast. He quickly moved it away, but she moved it back just as quickly.

"No one has ever touched me there except for my mother," she whispered, as he began to massage her through the layers of fabric. She moaned as a burning desire raced through her body. She felt herself becoming wet.

"We'd better get back," he said. "They're probably ready to head back to town. Papa said there were some things he wanted to ask about at the mercantile."

"Are you afraid of me?" she asked, squeezing his manhood.

"I'm afraid of us," he said.

"Chicken," she laughed. "You know something? We are wasting time. Would you like to go ahead with the wedding?"

"Don't get upset, but I would like for our first night be spent in our home," he said.

"That's romantic of you. What if I don't want to wait?"

"You'll have to," he said. "I'm the man and I'm boss."

"You just keep right on believing that darling. Loving you the way I've come to lately is changing me."

"In what way?"

"I'm not a girl anymore. I feel like I'm more than a just a girl."

"You were never just a girl, Angie."

"You were right," she said. "We had better go, this is getting heavy."

The family cabin...

"What have you two been doing?" Sophie asked.

"Not what you probably think. We've been daydreaming," Angie said. "Imagining what it's going to be like when we get all moved. Where we'll sleep; how long Jed can survive on mush. Important things like that."

"We lived on beans when we first got married, didn't, we hon?" Sophie asked.

"We did, and a lot of them were burned, but we couldn't afford to throw them away."

"You would remember that part," Sophie said, laughing.

"You're a good cook. How did you learn?" Angie asked.

"Trial and error, but mostly error. I actually learned from my grandmother when she came to stay with us after Grandpa passed. She insisted I do it, but she kept a close eye on everything."

"Seth ate a lot of mush when they first took me in and Polly was too sick to cook. To his credit, I never heard him complain."

"For Jed's sake, I guess we had better start my lessons," Angie said.

"You've got another month or so."

"We were talking about it earlier. We're wasting time, but he wants us to start off in our own home."

'It would be nice, but times change, and people change, like you did," Sophie reminded her.

CHAPTER TWENTY-FOUR

We Can Move

Back at the boarding house…

"Farmer's Bank has taken back a house abandoned by a man that left looking for gold," Hiram told his family. I arranged to buy the furnishings from the bank. I don't know what all it has, but the price was great and the bank was anxious to get some of their money back. I also opened an account with them."

"When can we see what you bought?" Sophie asked.

"It's getting late for today. We can go tomorrow morning."

The next day…

The house was furnished with the basics. The important items included a stove and beds. Everything was several years old, but in good condition.

"I can't help but wonder what happened to the family," Sophie said.

"The banker said they went back to Iowa after the man had been gone with no word for over a year."

"I hate to take advantage of someone's misfortune," she said.

"Honey, they're gone. No one lives here, so we're not booting them out. Let's just take a look. It might be the answer to Jed and Angie's needs."

"You're right. Let's take a look."

"It's used but serviceable," Sophie pronounced. "I would want to boil the bedding and kitchen things."

"Let's start getting it into the wagon," Hiram said. "We'll put the things going to your place in last," he told Jed. "We'll stop there first."

"This reminds me of our last day in Steubenville," Sophie told the others.

"We have enough to live here now," Angie told Jed after everything was unloaded.

"Not until we get the chinking done and the chimney completed. I'll show you what I'm talking about when we get to Papa's."

* * *

Jed carried the water and hauled dirt for the chinking process. Three walls were complete when he said, "Let's stop for the day." He looked at her and grinned. "Hold still. You've got mud on your face." He tried wiping it off with his sleeve, but only succeeded in smearing it.

"I'll just kiss it away," he said.

"If you start that, we might not get anything else done," she told him.

"It will be nice when we don't have to stop," he said.

"We don't have to now," she said, a big smile showing her perfect teeth.

"We do," he said. "I want it to be perfect."

"If you're ready to eat a lot of beans, let's pick a date to move."

"I'm up for that," he said. "Let's tell Mama."

The family cabin...

"Jed, they're going to start our fireplace and chimney tomorrow. I figure three days here and two at your place. We should both be able to move in a week.

"Mama, we want to have the wedding the day they finish the fireplace. Do you have anything you might need more time for?" Jed asked.

"What would I need more time for? I'm not the one getting married. I'm fine. I just wish we had a church and a preacher to conduct the ceremony to make it more memorable for Angie."

"My wedding day won't be a day I'll soon forget," Angie told her. "I would give anything to have Mom and Dad there. That's not going to happen and I've made peace with it."

* * *

Friday of the next week was picked as *the* day. It was Angie who came up with the best solution. Along with Jed, she went to the First United Methodist Church and spoke to the Reverend Stovall. "Reverend, we're new to Salem and we would like to get married," she said. "Would you perform the ceremony or can you refer us to someone?"

"I would be pleased to do so," he told them. "Have you found a church yet?"

"No sir. We came from Ohio and Missouri and have just claimed a homestead. We're staying at Mrs. Hinchley's Boarding House until our cabin is finished. We plan to move immediately after the wedding."

"My dear, are you now living in sin?" he asked.

"No sir. I was orphaned on the trail and Jed's parents and another family were kind enough to take me in."

"We would be pleased to have you join us whenever it is convenient to do so. We're a friendly congregation."

"Yes sir," she said.

"When would you like to take the vows?"

"Would Friday be convenient for you?" she asked.

"Yes, Friday will be fine."

"Good. It will be Jed's parents, his sister, the two of us and our neighbors. Thank you, Reverend Stovall."

CHAPTER TWENTY-FIVE

A Tragedy

The loud knocking on the door woke Sophie from a sound sleep. The knocking was punctuated by frantic calls of "Miss Sophie, Miss Sophie."

"Miss Sophie! Miss Sophie!" The panicked voice of Seth was muffled by the door. He knocked. "Miss Sophie!"

She opened the door. "What's wrong, Seth? Is it Polly?"

"Yes ma'am. Something's wrong. I'm afraid it's bad. Can you come?"

"I'll be right there. Hiram, get dressed and see if you can find a doctor."

She went down three doors to the Gilley's room. Polly was sobbing between the moans. "Put my hand where it hurts," Sophie said.

"Her belly and down there," Seth said.

"Is it steady or does it come and go?" The excruciating pain kept Polly from answering.

"It's steady now, but started out slow," Seth replied. "Is it the baby?"

"I don't know. It doesn't sound like it. Labor pains come and go. They get closer as the time comes. Hiram is going for the doctor."

It was almost an hour before Hiram knocked gently on the door, and stepped aside as an elderly, gray haired man came in carrying a black bag with the tools of his profession.

"I'm Doctor Phineas Barlow. What do we have here?" he asked. "Are you a midwife?"

"I'm just a friend and a mother. She said it's her belly and private area," Sophie said, as Polly screamed.

"If you gentlemen would wait outside while I examine the lady.

"Miss, I'll try to protect your modesty as much as possible," the doctor told Polly.

"Doctor, I think modesty is the least of Polly's problems right now," Sophie told him.

He pushed her protruding belly from side to side with his hands, each motion eliciting a scream. "I don't think this has anything to do with the baby. Her belly is extremely sensitive and warm. I do believe it is the appendix."

"Do we need to get her to your office?"

"I don't think she would survive the trip. Go to the kitchen. Wake Mrs. Hinchley and tell her I need some clean cloths and hot water. Be quick now. We don't have much time."

When Sophie returned, the doctor said, "I'm going to give her ether to knock her out. Then I'll go in and get this thing out. Can you help, or do I need to get Mrs. Hinchley?"

"I can do whatever you need. I'm a farmer's wife. I'm not squeamish."

"Good. Would you arrange her clothing to bare her waist and abdomen?"

She did as he requested. "Is this what you need?" she asked.

"Yes. That's good. I need for you to hold this over her nose and mouth. She may struggle until it begins to take effect, but keep it there, so I can drip more on it if she isn't sufficiently under. We don't want her waking up."

After fifteen minutes, he said, "I think she should be ready by now."

Mrs. Hinchley came in with a supply of white cloths. "Do you have the water heated, Clara?" he asked.

"I do. Is there anything else you need?"

"Not right now, this lady... What is your name, dear?"

"I'm Sophie Lewis."

"Mrs. Lewis is doing a fine job. Let me scrub my hands, and I'll get started."

Blood welled up in the three-inch incision he made in the lower right quadrant of Polly's belly and positioned a retractor to hold it open. Sophie turned her head to watch Polly when the cut was made. There was no indication of pain.

"I was afraid of this," Doctor Barlow said. "The appendix has ruptured." He removed the inflamed organ. I've used a lot of carbolic acid but in these cases, a rupture is usually fatal for the baby as well as the mother."

"What are you going to do next?" Sophie asked.

"I'm going to close the incision, and talk to the husband. He has a difficult decision to make."

"Let me get him while you do this," she requested.

She went out of the room. "She's going to be all right isn't she?" an anxious Seth asked about his wife.

"The doctor will be out in just a few minutes to talk to you.

"Hiram, I need to talk to you." He followed her down the hall.

"What is it?"

"Doctor Barlow doesn't think she's going to make it. Her appendix has ruptured. He said when this happens, it's almost always fatal for the mother and the baby."

"This will be a terrible blow to Seth. I don't know if I could take one like that, myself. What is the doctor going to tell Seth?"

"I don't know, but I think you should be there. They've been like our kids all this way. They're going to really need us now."

Back in the room...

"Son, your wife is seriously ill," the doctor began.

"How can having a baby make her seriously ill?" Seth asked.

"It wasn't the baby. Her appendix was infected and burst. It spread the infection all over her belly."

"She's going to be all right though, isn't she?"

"There's a chance. It's a small chance. In cases like this, it almost always means death for the mother and baby."

"Oh God, no," Seth wailed. Doc, I can't live without her. She's all I have. We didn't come all this far to have her die."

"As I said, she has a faint chance. Just in case the worse happens, you have a decision to make."

"What decision," Seth asked.

"If the infection gets into the blood stream, and it will, it could infect the baby. If that happens, in my opinion, your baby has no chance. I can deliver the baby now by cesarean and it has a good chance to survive. You have to give the permission."

"Can I see her now?" Seth asked.

"She's asleep now and probably will be for a few hours."

"Can I wait until she wakes?"

"Yes, but the longer you wait, there's a greater risk involved of blood poisoning."

"I'll wait."

Four hours later…

Polly began stirring.

CHAPTER TWENTY-SIX

She's Gone

Polly's eyes fluttered open. "I'm sorry to be so much trouble," Polly told her husband, smiling wanly. "It was bad, the worst pain I've ever had. Is our baby all right?"

"It wasn't the baby, honey. It was your appendix," Seth told her.

"Oh. Well, it's a lot better and doesn't hurt so bad now."

"Let's give them some privacy," Sophie said. "We'll be right outside."

It was quiet in the hallway. Then the sounds of crying came through the closed door. "He told her," Sophie said.

In the room…

"It was infected, and it burst. The doctor said the infection might spread or might not."

"What about my baby? Tell me. I have to know about my baby."

"He said if the infection gets to the baby, it probably won't make it. If he delivers it now, it should be all right."

"What about me? I'm going to die, aren't I?"

"We're all going to die someday, honey."

"Seth, stop beating around the bush and tell me the truth."

"Doctor Barlow said the infection is almost always too much, but there's a chance," the weeping Seth told his wife.

"I want to hold my baby before I die. Tell the doctor to save my baby."

He came out of the room. "She wants to have the baby now," he told his friends. "I'll tell the doctor."

"Is it all right if I go in?" Sophie asked.

"Yes, she'll want to see you."

"Miss Sophie, if I die, will you make sure my baby is taken care of? You have two good children. Will you make sure Seth takes good care of it and raises it right?"

"I will, but the doctor said you have a chance."

"If the worst happens, I'm worried about Seth. We're all each other has left. Our folks are all gone, and he'll be left alone."

"You're not alone and he won't be either. We're your family, so is Angie."

"We both love you, Miss Sophie. You've been like a mother to us."

"We love you too. You've been wonderful, good neighbors, and will continue to be. Seth's gone to tell the doctor. We'll be here for you."

Doctor Barlow delivered a healthy, five-pound-nine ounce baby girl. She was named Martha Sophronia, after her mother and her elected grandmother.

Three days later Polly grew restless. Her respiration rate increased and she had an elevated temperature. Doctor Barlow recommended she stop nursing. He found a wet nurse to feed the baby. Five days after delivery, Seth was holding an obviously deteriorating Polly in his arms when she began talking.

"I'm dying Seth." He started to say something, but she stopped him. "No, let me talk. I want you to promise you will take care of our baby. I want you to promise you will find a good mother for her and wife for you to love, one who will be a good mother. Promise me Seth."

He didn't respond, and she tightened her grip on his hand. "Promise me. You have to promise so I can go in peace. Promise."

His voice choking, he said, "I promise."

"One other thing. I want to be buried on our land. We went through so much to get here. I want to be where I can watch over you and Martha."

That evening, with Seth, Sophie, Hiram, Angie, Jed and Mandy by her bedside, she took her last breath in the arms of her weeping husband.

"Seth, she was one of the bravest people I ever knew," Sophie told him "Her struggles with being with child and traveling every day were met with a strength few people have, yet I never heard her complain."

"She was still young. If we had stayed home, this wouldn't have happened. It's my fault for making her take the trip."

"You can't blame yourself. A lot of people have appendicitis. It can happen anywhere. No one knows why she was called home so young. So many people died trying to make a new life for themselves. She survived all of that and gave you a fine baby girl in her last act on earth. You have the responsibility to take care of her now."

The next day, Polly was laid to rest near where their cabin would be built.

Jed and Hiram were filling the grave. Sophie rested her hand on Seth's shoulder. "Martha can stay with us until you get settled. We'll take good care of her. You come over anytime you want. She's going to need her papa to love her. Is that all right with you?"

The sobbing man didn't say anything. "Seth, is that all right with you?" she asked again.

He nodded.

"I expect to see you soon, Seth."

Another nod. The grave was filled. Hiram knelt beside Seth. "It's a loss no man should have to face," he told Seth. "You don't have to face it alone. We loved Polly too."

Seth looked up. "I'd like to be alone with my wife."

Hiram nodded. "We'll be going back to town then. You know where we'll be when you need us." He stood, and patted the distraught man on the back. "We're sorry you have to go through this." He returned to his family.

"He's in a bad way," Hiram told his wife. "I would hate to go through what he's facing now. With a baby too. It's almost too much to ask of any man."

"I told him we'd take care of Martha until he gets settled," Sophie said. "We can make room for the wet nurse until he's ready to take her. It's a responsibility he's going to have to pick up though. The sooner the better."

"He's in no shape to do that now," Hiram said.

No one had seen Seth all week when Friday, the day of the wedding came.

CHAPTER TWENTY-SEVEN

A Wedding

First United Methodist Church, Salem…

It was 11:00AM when the Lewis family met at the church. They were joined by several of the regular members of the congregation.

"I'm Thomas Stovall, pastor of the church, and I'm happy to see you here this morning.

"We are gathered to unite Miss Angela Thornton and Mr. Jedadiah Lewis in Holy Matrimony. I've met with this young couple and have found they satisfy the tenets of the church and it is my honor and privilege to conduct the ceremony. Let us proceed."

Angie was wearing her best dress, and carried a small bouquet of flowers picked that morning by Jed. She carried a Bible that had belonged to Polly Gilley.

Reverend Stovall read from his book of rituals and said, "Please join hands."

Jed took her hand and fixed his eyes on her radiant face as the minister asked him to repeat the vow. "Do you Jedadiah, take this woman, Angela to be your lawful wedded wife, to have and to hold, for richer or for poorer, in sickness and in health, forsaking all others, so long as you both shall live?"

Jed in a strong voice said, "I do."

"Do you Angela, take this man, Jedadiah to be your lawful wedded husband, to have and to hold, for richer or for poorer, in sickness and in health, forsaking all others, so long as you both shall live?"

"I do."

"By the powers vested in me by the Lord God Almighty and the great state of Oregon, I pronounce you man and wife.

"Jedadiah, you may kiss your bride."

It was a soft, tender kiss, one that ended with a whispered, "I love you, Angie Lewis."

"I love you too, Jed."

"Please join with me as I ask for the blessings of the Lord to rain down on you both and on your marriage," After the prayer, he said, "May I be the first to congratulate you and offer my best wishes?"

"Thank you Reverend Stovall. We appreciate your making time for us," Angie said.

"I guess I'm now officially part of your family," she told Sophie.

"You have been a part of our family since you got here."

Mandy hugged her. "You are the nicest thing that's happened to our family since I was born," she said laughing.

"I wouldn't agree with that, maybe the second nicest, after Jed."

"You're talking about my brother?"

"No, I was thinking about my husband."

"I sort of hoped Seth would be here. I guess it's still too soon. No one's seen him have they?"

"Mrs. Hinchley told me this morning the room hasn't been used. I will pack their stuff and take it with us. There's no point in keeping the room if he doesn't use it.

"Tonight will be our last night here. Where are you and Jed staying?"

"We will be at our farm," Angie said, "and the latch string will definitely not be out."

"Honey, I just thought of something, two things we should do while we're in town," Jed said. "We need to go by the land office and file a claim in your name, and the other is we need to go by the mercantile and pick up some things in case we want to eat."

"Good idea," Angie said. "I'm so excited I forgot about it."

"I'll help you with that part of it," Sophie said. "I doubt you have much experience in it. By the way, you're having supper with us tonight," Sophie told them. "It's not open for discussion. Now, if you'll excuse me, I need to get started packing."

"I'll pack Polly and Seth's room," Angie said. "I don't think there's much in there."

"I'll help," Mandy offered.

"You help Mama, it won't take me long. My things are already packed.

Later...

"Jed, I'm ready to go to the Land Office whenever you are."

An hour later, the addition of another section of land was made to Jed's original claim. "Our farm is now larger than the one we had in Steubenville," he told her.

"I imagine it's larger than our dairy farm was too," Angie told him. "Let's get back to the boarding house so we can help get everything loaded up."

"Papa, we need to get another wagon," Jed told his father.

"You're right. We already have the oxen and horses to pull it. Let's go down to the livery and see what we can find."

The used wagon they purchased needed repairs on the floor and sideboards. It had been poorly maintained, but the price was low. Jed would pick it up the next Monday.

The ladies were ready to go when they returned to the boarding house. It was time to move to their farms.

When they arrived at the main cabin, Jed said, "Let's unload the things you're going to use here and then we'll leave after supper."

After supper...

Angie went inside with Sophie and once inside, they moved away from the door. In a quiet voice, Sophie said, "This may be a little embarrassing for you, but I'm the closest thing you have to a mother now, so I'm going to tell you about it. You were raised on a dairy farm, so you know how things work. The first time is going to hurt a good bit, but it won't last long. There will be some blood, but don't worry about it. After the first or second time, it can be downright pleasurable."

"It's not embarrassing. Mom and I had the talk when I first started high school, but she didn't talk about this part. I'm glad you brought it up. I never would have."

Jed's voice came from the outside. "Angie, are you ready?"

"I am now," she replied, and smiled at Sophie.

* * *

Angie stepped onto the wheel and hopped to the ground in front of their cabin. "Wait, don't go in yet," Jed said.

"You need my help?"

"Sort of." He scooped her into his arms and carried her to the door. She giggled all the way. "Can you get the latchstring?"

"I think I can manage it."

He lowered her to the floor. "I'll get the rest of the things and take care of the horses. Don't go away."

"I promise."

CHAPTER TWENTY-EIGHT

After the Wedding

She lit a coal oil lamp. He came back inside, and looked around nervously. He shuffled his feet, then went back to the door and pulled the latchstring inside.

It was the first time they had been shy together since they first met two thousand miles back.

"Are you uncomfortable about this?" Jed asked.

"Uncomfortable is not what I feel. Scared would be a better word. We took a big step into a new beginning that will last for the rest of our lives. After my parents died, I had to face the fact I was alone. Fortunately, some wonderful people came along that helped me face it. Now I'm married with a husband I'm responsible for, and I don't know how to go about it." She wrung her hands nervously. "I would say I'm nervous. I'm afraid I'll make a mistake and mess things up."

He took her in his arms, and pulled her into a tight embrace. He tilted her head back and looked into her emerald green eyes. "If mistakes are made, then we'll face them and fix them together. Don't be afraid."

"I am a nervous to tell the truth. Marriage came at a lot younger age than I expected."

He searched her face for signs of doubt. "I don't want you to be nervous. Why don't I just put my bedroll on the floor in front of the fireplace until you feel okay with us together?"

"That's not what I'm talking about. I love you and want to be with you. I'm totally inexperienced and I'm afraid I'll disappoint you."

The grin spread across his face. "I love you too much to ever be disappointed in you, honey. In any way."

Her voice quavered a little shaky when she asked, "Would you help me with this?"

His fingers trembled, as he slowly unbuttoned the top buttons of her dress. He felt her shiver through his fingers. "We're going to have a good life," he said. "I'm going to try my best to help you make up for what you've lost.

The unbuttoned dress was pushed off her shoulders and fell to the floor. The next layer followed the first. "My turn now," she said and began to unbutton his shirt. Unable to resist the temptation, she slid her hands inside the partially undone shirt and wrapped her arms around his chest.

"Um… You're a lot more muscular than you look. This makes me go weak in the knees."

He shrugged the shirt off, and let it fall to the floor, and then pulled the cotton undershirt over his head and flung it aside. She buried her face in his neck. Her warm breath on his neck sent waves of desire raging through his entire body.

She looked into the dark pools of his eyes, and removed her chemise. He pulled her to his chest and heard her sharp intake of breath when her breasts touched his bare chest. He felt the tips of her nipples singe the hairs on his pectoral muscles.

"Take me to bed," she whispered.

"Are you sure?" he asked.

"That's your silly question of the day. I have never been as sure of anything as I am of this."

He turned the wick of the lamp down until the light faded, and returned to the bed. He removed his trousers and underwear. When he pushed the quilt down, his fingers brushed her breast, he recoiled as if he had touched a hot poker. "I'm sorry," he said.

She found his hand and moved back to her breast. "There. Isn't that better?"

"Yes. Oh yes, much better." His voice was two octaves lower than normal. His mouth covered hers hungrily as she pressed against him. He realized she had removed the rest of her clothing.

When they broke the kiss, he said, "The day we found you, was the luckiest day of my life."

"I'm glad it was your family who found me." She slid her hand down his chest and over his belly. She felt him tense when she touched his member. She let out a low moan that grew louder as his hand found the entrance to her treasure vault.

A river of wetness washed over his fingers as he inserted first one and then a second finger inside stretching the walls. Her body began moving against his hand involuntarily. The moans grew louder and louder and she increased the movements of her hips. Then she lost all control and began thrusting upward, harder and harder until a long sigh escaped and she was still.

"Honey, are you all right?" he asked.

She didn't answer at first, and then said, "Wow. That was the most incredible feeling I have ever had. I don't see how it can get any better, but I'm ready to try the next part."

She pulled him on top and guided him to the entrance. He felt the resistance. "Push," she told him.

He pushed against the resistance. The pain was sharp and intense. Her scream was involuntary and she forced herself to relax as she slowly exhaled.

He stopped moving and began to withdraw.

"Don't stop. It's not as bad as it was," she said. "I expected it to hurt at first."

Later…

"We are truly a married couple now," she said.

"It's kind of scary isn't it?" he replied.

"It is scary," she agreed. "Here we are married and both of us are just eighteen. What do we know about anything other than we love each other? What if that isn't enough?

"What if we just made a baby?"

"Then it will be the most loved baby in the state of Oregon. As much as I love you, love will be enough," he promised.

"We're going to be all right. We have a nice sized farm and we'll have a crop of wheat in the spring. Best of all, we have each other."

"I don't know why I've gotten to be such a worry wart," she said. "I never was before. I had responsibilities to the other players on the teams and didn't want to let them down, but this seems to be so much more. It bothers me that we will be so dependent on your family until we can begin growing our own food. You know how I am about having to depend on someone when I have nothing to offer in return."

"With three cows there will be plenty of milk, and we may have to eat a lot of mush and beans."

"That's all right with me. I can help with the milking. I can also cook mush. Beans can't be all that hard to cook.

"Jed?" she said, running her fingers through the sparse hairs on his chest. "I would kind of like to try it again."

"Your wish is my command," he said.

Later…

"Mm, that felt good. A lot easier than the first time." She lay back on his outstretched arm and snuggled her chin into the space between his shoulder and chin. "I'm going to like being married. Goodnight, Jed."

"Good night, honey."

CHAPTER TWENTY-NINE

Where's Seth?

The next week…

Angie picked Martha up from her rocking cradle. "Isn't she beautiful?" she asked.

"She is, and she looks so much like Polly, it is unreal."

"How often does Seth come to see her?"

"We haven't seen him since the funeral," Sophie said.

"He hasn't even been here to see his daughter?" Angie asked.

"Not one time."

"Something has to be done about this," Angie said. "I promised Polly I would help look after Martha, and I keep my promises. I'll get Jed to take me to see him."

"Honey, let Hiram talk to him. There's no telling what he might do if you try to force him to accept Polly's gone and he has a daughter."

* * *

Hiram saddled his horse and rode to Seth's homestead. "We haven't seen much of you lately, so I came to see how you're doing," Hiram said.

"As well as can be expected for somebody that lost everything," Seth replied.

"You haven't lost everything, you have a daughter," Hiram reminded him.

"No way I can take care of a child," Seth said. "I've got to put seed in the ground. I'm living in the wagon. I can't very well take care of a baby while I'm plowing."

"You could at least visit her. You haven't seen her in two months. You know we've moved in, and we're just the next farm over."

"Yeah, well I couldn't hire a bunch of Chinese to do my work. I have to do the work myself."

Hiram ignored the sarcasm. "Do you think Polly would like to see you like this? Didn't you promise to take care of her baby? We weren't in the room, but we could hear what was said. She would be ashamed of what you've become."

"You got no call talking to me like this," Seth said, angrily.

"Go down to the creek and look at yourself. You're filthy and I can smell you over here. Get hold of yourself man, you're not the first person to lose his wife. We're getting mighty attached to Martha, and she's a happy baby. If you don't want her, we'd be more than happy to adopt her."

He wheeled his horse around and called back over his shoulder, "You know where we live if you decide to visit."

Saturday afternoon…

Seth called, "Hello the house!"

Sophie came to the door. "Seth, this is a pleasant surprise!" She turned and called over her shoulder, "Mandy, we have a visitor. Come in, I've got a pot of coffee on."

"Would it be all right if I visited Martha?" he asked.

"Well of course it would. She's probably still asleep, but I'll get her up to see her papa."

When she returned, she said, "I had to change her. Martha, your papa has come to see you." She thrust the baby at Seth, leaving him no choice but to take her.

"I'm afraid I might drop her," he said.

"Nonsense. Take the rocker. She loves to be rocked."

"Where are the others?" Seth asked.

"Hiram and Jed are working on their cabin."

"What about Angie?"

Mandy answered, "Angie and Jed live on their farm."

"They married?" he asked.

"They did, and they are as happy as hogs in fresh mud. I didn't hold out a lot of hope it would happen for a while there. Angie's a very pretty girl and there are a lot of men looking for a wife," she continued. "I was afraid he might dawdle around and lose her.

"I'm going to start looking around for myself," Mandy said.

Both Seth and Sophie had surprised looks on their faces. "Why are you looking at me like that, Mama?" Mandy asked.

"It's just not something you've said before. I would be very happy if you found some nice young man. It seemed for a while like you might be my last chance for another grandbaby to go along with Martha, but now with Jed and Angie there's renewed hope."

"How are you doing, Seth?" Mandy asked.

"I miss her every day. I keep hoping this is a bad dream and she will walk in with her usual smile, and everything will be fine."

"I miss her too. I counted her among my best friends. Angie took it as hard as the rest of us.

"How is your cabin coming along?"

He looked at his daughter. "I'm embarrassed to say I haven't done a thing with it. I'm living in the wagon. I did get the seed for winter wheat in the ground, but my heart just is not in it.

"Would it be all right if I came to see my daughter?"

"Now that is the dumbest question I've heard all day," Sophie told him. Of course it will. Why don't you come tomorrow for Sunday dinner?"

"I've promised myself I will start working on some shelter. I had better be getting back now," he said. "I'm going to try to get some more work in today."

"Seth, don't be a stranger. The latchstring is always out for you."

"Thank you, Sophie. I appreciate what you're doing for Martha."

"She's a little darling. And she looks just like her mother."

"Do you think so?"

"Just look at her eyes and the shape of her face. She's her mother's daughter all right."

Later…

"Guess who was here today?" Sophie asked when Jed and Hiram came in.

"Seth came over. He held Martha and talked to her. I have never seen a sadder person. Do you know he hasn't done anything toward building shelter?"

"I saw that the other day. I'm not surprised," Hiram said. "He was the filthiest one human I've ever seen when I was over there."

"He was all cleaned up today. Shaved and everything. He does need help. Why don't you and Jed go help get him started? It would be the neighborly thing to do. I'll fix lunch. I don't think he's had a decent meal since he left the boarding house."

"Let's do that," Hiram said. "It would be nice if we had some neighbors. We could have an old fashioned wall raising."

"That would be nice," Sophie said. "It was always done through the church. The next time we go into Salem, I want to see whether there are any in the area. I miss that."

"We'll need to go in next week," Hiram said. "Get a list together of what you need. I need some nails. I want to finish flooring the loft and build a lean-to for another room."

"Angie asked me if we decorated the house for Christmas. We never have before, but she had some suggestions using colored paper and popcorn strings. I think Jed is going to take her and Mandy to look for a tree. It would be nice to have one for our first Christmas here. I am going to ask Seth to have Christmas dinner with us too."

CHAPTER THIRTY

A Confrontation

They found the perfect tree. Six feet tall and well filled out on all sides. "This is going to be perfect," Angie told them. Jed loaded it into the back of the wagon and they headed home.

Jed nailed boards onto the base of the tree so it would stand. They picked a spot in a corner, away from the fireplace. Angie and Mandy began cutting strips of colored paper to make chains of rings, while Sophie popped the popcorn and made a flour paste to glue the paper strips into rings.

They made strings from the popped popcorn and the girls strung them on the tree along with the colored rings. "The only thing we need is an ornament for the top," Angie told them.

Jed and Hiram pronounced it beautiful when they returned from their work in the barn.

Christmas day…

Sophie served dinner at 2:00PM. Crowded around the table were seven people including Martha. Angie greeted Seth warmly and sat next to him at the table. "I haven't seen you in months. How are you doing?"

"Not too well," he replied. "I can't seem to get anything done. I just can't concentrate long enough to get anything beyond starting."

"Come with me," she said, and led him to the cradle Hiram had made. "Look at what you and Polly did together. You created this little human being. Concentrate on her."

"It's all I can do to look at her. She looks so much like Polly, I can't stand it."

"Don't you think that's what God intended? He took Polly but left you something just as precious. She's more dependent on you than Polly was. She needs her father."

"Hiram and Sophie are taking far better care of her than I ever could," he said.

"They are forty years older than she is. They are like her grandparents. I stayed with my grandparents one summer, and I could hardly wait to get back to Mom and Dad."

"It's different. You knew them. She doesn't know me."

"Whose fault is that? She can't ride a horse or hitch a wagon. She can't even talk to ask someone to take her to see her father. Don't you want her?"

"It's not that," he said. "It's…"

"If you don't want her, tell me. Jed and I will take her and raise her as our own. Come on Seth. You and Polly took me in when I had nothing. I loved her and I admired you. No longer. If you want to be rid of Polly's daughter, say the word and come to the courthouse tomorrow. Jed and I will meet you there. We can file for adoption and you'll be rid of her and all of this responsibility you have that you don't want to face.

"It's a good thing Polly isn't here to see the way you are treating the little girl that she carried through so much pain and hurt.

"Yes, I said pain and hurt. She never let you see it, but she told me about it when she was so sick on the trail. She told me how she hoped the baby would wait to be born in her new home. She was so afraid she was going to die without giving this little girl a chance to live. She was able to hold her, once or twice, and I'll bet she died happier for it. You don't deserve either one of them.

"She made me promise to help look after Martha. Now, do we meet you in the courthouse tomorrow or not?"

Hiram came to where they were standing. "Is there anything wrong?"

Angie looked up and smiled. "No, nothing's wrong. Seth is struggling with a decision he has to make. I'm going to see if I can help Mama."

"You look as if you ran into a wall," Hiram said.

"It was a wall named Angie. She let me have it with both barrels."

"About what?"

"What else? Martha. She said if I didn't want her, then I should meet her and Jed at the courthouse and they'd adopt her on the spot."

"Are you going to meet them?"

"No. I have to do what I promised Polly I would do. Did you know about this?"

"No, and I doubt Jed does either. The happiest day of his life was the day they married. She's something special, that girl," Hiram said.

"Just like that day on the raft. She didn't even stop to think, but went into the water after Mandy. We are all glad she is part of our family."

"We loved her too. She took good care of Polly. She apparently was sicker than she ever let on to me. I will keep my promise to her. I'm going to advertise for a bride. Who could refuse my 'I live in a lean-to and I have a three month old baby girl' advertisement?"

Hiram laughed. "It does have a certain ring to it. Unless they're in town adopting a daughter, we'll be over tomorrow."

Later…

"I need to be going," Seth said. "I've got a lot of work to do." He lifted his daughter from her cradle. "You do look like your mama, baby girl, and I do love you." He put her back in the cradle. "You're going to outgrow that. I need to get to work on a crib."

He told everyone goodbye, but Angie hugged him. "Will we see you tomorrow?" she whispered.

"If you come to my place, you will. I won't be at the courthouse."

"Good. I'm not sure how good our parenting skills would be, but we would love her. She is that important to me."

"I believe you, and thanks, Angie. I owe you."

"No, you owe Martha and Polly."

Later…

"Seth told me what you told him," Hiram said. "I think he believed you."

"It wasn't a bluff, Mr. Hiram. I would have. I made Polly a promise too, and I intend to keep mine."

"Well, you won't have to follow through. He's going to advertise for one of them mail order brides. There's no one around here for him that I know about.

"Jed and I are going to help him finish out his cabin. We're going over tomorrow to help make it livable."

"There is one girl," Angie said. "You forgot about Mandy. He's only a year or two older."

"Mandy's not interested in getting married," he told her.

"I wouldn't bet the farm on that if I were you."

"Not Mandy. You're kidding, right?"

That evening…

"Has Mandy said anything about getting married?" Hiram asked Sophie after they had gone to bed.

"We've talked a bit about it, but no one in particular, why?"

"Angie gave Seth a real talking to, even told him if he didn't want Martha, then she and Jed would meet him at the courthouse and they'd adopt her."

"She didn't!"

"She did and she told me she meant it. Anyway, Seth told me he ain't going to do it, and said he's going to advertise for a wife.

"I mentioned it to her and she said he didn't have to, Mandy's here. When I told her Mandy wasn't interested in marriage, she told me not to bet on it. That girl is something else. I'd hate to get sideways with her."

"She told me she's not sure she's mature enough to be a mother. She's a lot more mature than she thinks. She's going to make a good wife for Jed and they are going to be very happy together."

CHAPTER THIRTY-ONE

A New Beginning

Mandy and Angie were removing the decorations from the tree. "What do we do with these?" Mandy asked.

"We should probably burn the rings," Angie said. "The popcorn would smell pretty bad if we burned it. We can't feed it to the animals because of the thread we used to string it together. I guess if we threw it in the chicken pen, they would eat it."

"What about the tree?"

"Let Jed drag it out into the field and just let it decay. They do make a spectacular fire, but that might not be such a good idea."

"I'm glad you suggested we do this. It has made it one of our best Christmases ever," Mandy told her.

"I snuck some pictures of the tree," Angie told her. "They will give me something to look at and remember over the winter. My iPhone is not going to hold out forever and when it's gone it can't be repaired. I might as well get all of the enjoyment I can."

"What will you do when it dies?"

"Cry. It's the only thing I have to remind me of Mom and Dad."

"That is so sad," Mandy told her.

"Can we talk about something else?"

"What was it like flying in those things that went so fast?" Mandy asked.

"Most of the time, it's just like sitting in a chair. If you look out the window, it's hard to tell you're moving because you're so high, except when you're landing."

"How high?

"Thirty-five thousand feet. That would be six or seven miles.

"I would be so scared I would probably wet myself," Mandy said.

Angie laughed. "They have bathrooms where you do that. A lot of people are afraid to fly, but just think, as far as you traveled in seven months, you could go in four or five hours."

"Now that would be nice, but we wouldn't have been able to see you in the tree from that high up."

"Jeremy would have found me. His curiosity never ends."

"I'm glad you're here with us, but I wish there had been an easier way for you to do it."

"So do I. My feet are still tired."

"That's not what I meant, and you know it," Mandy said. She pulled Angie into an embrace and held her. "I love you. My whole family loves you."

"If you try to kiss me, I'll slug you. I love all of you too. And, I'm grateful to you too. Now let's drag this tree out of here."

"You sound just like your husband."

When they went back inside, Angie said, "Look at the needles on the floor. Mama is going to be all over us. I'll get the broom."

Sophie came from the bedroom while Angie was sweeping. "I just swept this morning."

"It made a mess when we dragged the tree out. I thought I'd better get it cleaned up before you saw it and got mad."

"It's a good thing you did. I can be mean when I'm riled." Her smile showed she was joking.

"I know, Jed told me."

"He's certainly been on the receiving end enough to know."

"I was always the good child," Mandy said.

"You got your share of it too, little girl."

"Speaking of little girls, has Seth been to see his little one since Christmas?" Angie asked.

"He was here yesterday," Sophie said. "He even looked a little better. Hiram said he will have a livable place in another week or two.

"He told me yesterday he has put an advertisement in the Matrimonial News for a wife."

"I didn't know that," Mandy said.

"Why don't you answer the ad?" Angie asked Mandy.

"I can't answer it if I don't see it."

"Oh come on Mandy, there are ways. The next time we go to town, we can see if the mercantile knows anything about it. Where would it come from anyway?"

"I imagine the one in this area would come from San Francisco," Sophie said. "There was a man on our train that told us it was published in three places. I would guess you have to get it in the mail though.

"I didn't know you were that interested in getting married," her mother said. Your pa and I were talking about it the other night.

"Of course I would like to get married," Mandy said. "It's just we don't have too many unmarried men coming around here."

"You have one," Angie pointed out.

"He's still grieving for Polly."

"He has a daughter that needs a mother. That should speed up the process," Angie said. "You would be a good mother for Martha."

"You've been sweeping that same spot for ten minutes. I think you've gotten all of the needles by now," Mandy said.

"I'm thinking."

"Don't go matchmaking for me, Angie."

"Seems to me I said something just like that to you a while back. Why shouldn't I? You kept at me about Jed until I finally gave in. The least I can do is return the favor."

"Seth probably thinks of me as a young girl, not as a woman."

"You don't know that. If he opens his eyes and takes a good look at your figure, he'll know you're not a little girl."

"My figure?" Mandy asked.

"Yes, your figure. Your butt, and your boobs are not those of a little girl."

"That's almost scandalous you thinking that way," Mandy said.

"You mean to tell me you've never looked at yourself in the mirror when you have no clothes on? I certainly look at myself." Mandy's face colored, because she had done the same.

"All girls do. The honest ones admit it," Angie said.

"So do older women," Sophie said. "I want to be attractive for my husband."

"This conversation is getting beyond embarrassing," Mandy said. "Seth has never…"

"He was happily married, and now he's not anymore," Angie said. "He's a good man. If you're interested, don't let him get away."

Later…

"Angie, do you really think I should set my cap for him?"

"Now you know no one can answer that for you. You're talking about something that would affect three people for the rest of their lives… You, Seth, and Martha.

"Listen to me giving advice to someone two years older than I am."

"This is the reason I always wanted a sister so I'd have someone to talk with about things like this."

"I'll say it again. If you're interested, don't let him get away. You can see how happy I am married to Jed. I have hope and I'm looking forward to the future."

"If you could go back now, would you?"

"I think I would under two conditions. One would be if Jed could go too. If he couldn't, I would go only if I was sure I could come back here.

"There's no point talking about it. I can't go, and I'm happy now. That's what counts."

"You never know. Strange things do happen," Mandy said.

"Especially around me," Angie said.

The End… (for now)

Epilogue

Angie and Jed had four children, two boys and two girls. The oldest daughter was named Alexandra after Angie's mother, and the youngest was Sophronia for her paternal grandmother. Their oldest child, Hiram, was named for his grandfather. The youngest boy was named Jedadiah after his father.

The Lewis farms were a financial success, and were combined into one when taken over by Jedadiah after his father decided to retire. Jed passed away in 1920, and was followed by Angie in 1925.

When Angie passed, her daughters, Sophie and Martha arranged the funeral. When they sorted through her possessions, they found the small pink, rectangular object they had seen their mother holding many times. Neither knew what the object was, and when they asked about it, their mother told them it had been a Christmas gift from her father.

The two girls decided to put it in the coffin with their mother. She was buried in the Lewis family cemetery.

Mandy's story will be chronicled in a sequel to Angie and the Farmer.

In 1937, portions of the original farm were taken by eminent domain process to be used as a school site. Almost all of the graves in the family cemetery were relocated to another part of the farm... It was almost all, because one was missed.

If you liked "Angie and the Farmer", a review would be very much appreciated.

Excerpts

The following pages are excerpts from other books in the Oregon Trail Time Travel Romance Series.

You are invited to visit my website, <u>Susan Leigh Carlton</u> for more information. You are also invited to sign up for my reader's list where you can receive unedited, pre-publish first chapters of my new books. I do not spam, nor do I sell email addresses. You have the option to unsubscribe at any time.

Thank you for your interest in my efforts.

Susan Leigh Carlton

ROMANCE IN TIME

The deafening crack of thunder startled her; followed by a spectacular flash of sparks and flame as the bolt of lightning split a tall Ponderosa pine down the middle leaving both halves smoking; and their branches consumed in flames. Momentarily blinded, Abby swerved and lost control of her Subaru. Even though she was buckled in, she felt the sensation of flying through the air. She could see the ground beneath her, so she knew she was not in a car. She flew through a wall of blackness and found herself in the middle of nowhere.

No highway, no buildings, just the two men on horseback. And what seemed like an endless stream of wagons, some pulled by oxen, others by horses. Most of the animals were controlled by men who walked along side. Some wagons had women on the seat, while others had women walking alongside. They all looked weary, not a smile on any of them. Small children peeked out of the arched coverings in the rear of the wagons. The dust kicked up by the hundreds of hooves and wheels hung over the wagons like a low hanging tan cloud.

The man in the brown duster, who looked to be about forty-five, was astride a dun colored horse, asked, "Miss, what are you doing outchere all by yourself? If one of the Lakota raiding parties had found you instead of us, there ain't no telling what they'da done. Did you get lost from one of the trains on up ahead of us? I ain't seen you on ours before."

"No," Abby replied. "I wasn't on a wagon. I don't know how I got here."

"You don't know or you don't remember?" the previously silent man said, pulling the reins of his large roan horse, causing it to back up. He was wearing jeans, a denim shirt, and a wide brimmed hat. He had a stubble on his chin with dark curly hair touching his collar.

"I don't know," she said. "Lightning struck a tree; I lost control and here I am."

"Your horse throwed you?" the first man asked.

"I didn't have a horse, and I don't know how I got here."

"Well, you didn't just fall out of the sky," the older man said.

"I don't think I did either, but I don't have an explanation," Abby replied.

"Jack, I think she's likely been in the sun too long," the older man said.

"What's your name, ma'am?" Jack asked.

"Abigail Sanders."

"I'm Caleb Watson, the wagon master. This here's Jack Calhoun. He'll take you back to the preacher's wagon; we've got to keep moving if we're going to make it to the next water before dark." He waved his arm in a circle over his head, signaling the wagons to begin rolling.

"Sir... Mr. Watson, I was going home to my grandfather's ranch outside Laramie. How can I get there?"

"I don't rightly know. We must be fifty or sixty miles from Fort Laramie. We can't turn around and go back. That'd be three days or more, and we can't spare the time."

"Not Fort Laramie, Just Laramie. I had been to the fort and was going back home."

Jack helped her onto the horse behind him. "Hold on, Miss Sanders, I don't know how far back the preacher's wagon is. You'll like them. They're nice people."

BELLE OF THE BALL

Anna was in the Ladies Room when the lights flickered. She quickly took note of where she was in the room in case they went out. The shaking increased in intensity. Water sloshed from the toilets. The lights flickered, then went out. With her hand on the wall for orientation, she made her way to the door. Surely the emergency lights in the hall would be on.

They weren't. A ceiling beam had fallen and blocked the exit to the ballroom. She remembered the instructions from some long past school lecture and stood in the doorway. It was pitch black in front of her as well as behind. She could touch both sides of the doorway, so she decided to stay put, and started to sit down. Sliding her hand down the doorframe as a guide, it reached the bottom and felt water. *So much for that.* She couldn't sit.

An explosion rocked the building as a ruptured gas line ignited. Anna was thrown back against the wall. A piece of the falling ceiling struck her on the head. On the verge of panic, she heard a soft voice say, "Follow me. I'll show you the way. You can't help them now." She saw a woman in a long, flowing white dress.

"How? I can't see anything. It's as black as a cave."
Then, off to her right, she saw a faint glow as the
woman walked down the hall to her right.

"Follow the light," the soft voice said again.

Her hand touching the wall, she stood, and moved
slowly forward toward the only thing she could see, the
pale glow surrounding the woman.

The glow became brighter, but she still couldn't see
the end of the hall. The brilliance of the light was far
greater than she had ever seen. "Don't be afraid," the
voice said. "You're near the end, and I am with you."

*I'm dying. There's no pain. Can you die without
pain? Lord, let mom and dad know I didn't suffer. I
should have died when the train hit the bus. I knew it.*

"My work here isn't finished and this is where I
leave you. Go through the door. All will be well." The
glow and the woman vanished, leaving her in the
stygian blackness.

Anna felt for a knob, found it and turned it. She
pushed against the knob and the door swung open
easily. She stepped through and looked to her left… and
fainted.

The water from the damp cloth on her forehead ran
into her hair. Where am I?"

"You're in my office. I'm Doctor Carter Palmer; this
is my wife, Elizabeth. Do you know what happened to
you?"

"I was in the Ladies Room and everything started shaking. I guess it was an earthquake. I waited until it stopped. It was black and I couldn't see. The normal way out was blocked and someone led me out another way. I went out through the door and looked around. That's all I remember."

"You were found at the end of an alley and they brought you to my office."

"Why didn't they take me to the ER?" she asked.

"I don't understand," Carter said.

"The emergency room at the hospital, in the ambulance."

"Miss… excuse me, I don't even know your name."

"I'm Anna Reeves."

"Anna, there is no hospital in Helena. I'm the only doctor in town."

Panic filled her face. "I was born in the hospital in Helena. They fixed my broken wrist there. I don't know what's going on. Call my mother and dad right now or I'll call the police."

"Miss Reeves, I'll send someone for your parents," Carter assured her. "I'll send for the sheriff if you like. We don't have a police department."

ABOUT THE AUTHOR

Susan Leigh Carlton lives just outside Tomball, Texas, a suburb twenty-six miles northwest of Houston. She began writing and publishing on Amazon in August of 2012.

Susan observed the eighty-second anniversary of her birth on April 17th. She says, "I quit having birthdays, because they are depressing." Susan and her husband celebrated their fiftieth wedding anniversary on April 16th, 2016, the day before her birthday.

Susan has said many times, "One of the joys I get from writing is the emails I receive from readers that have read and liked my books. I even like the letters that are critical of the writing because it means the writer cared enough to take the time to write.

Visit my website at www.susanleighcarlton.com and sign up to receive advance copies of the first chapter when I start a new book.

Susan's Website
Amazon's Susan Leigh Carlton's Sales Page

Made in United States
Troutdale, OR
10/30/2023

14150770R00120